BEYOND DUTY

Love on the Double Series

Book 2

L.A. REMENICKY

Lavish
Publishing LLC

Contents

Chapter One

PREOCCUPIED with his friend Rina's problems and a lack of sleep the previous night, Jessie Monroe didn't notice the car off to the side of the road until he had driven past it. A glance in his rearview mirror showed him the curvy butt and long legs of a female bent over and rummaging in the trunk of the car. With a quick three-point turn, he pulled his truck up behind the disabled vehicle.

He grinned when he heard a voice yelling from the back of the car. "Dammit! How in the hell am I supposed to change a tire with no jack?" The trunk slammed shut, and he could now see the front of the woman as she looked toward the sky and screamed, "Why me?"

Jessie ambled toward the blonde. "Hey there. Need some help?" He had to remind himself to breathe when he noticed her eyes, molten chocolate burning with emotion. Looking her up and down, he wondered where such a beauty came from.

"My eyes are up here, soldier," she said with a smirk when his gaze stopped at her chest. "I am more than just my boobs."

1

Jessie looked up. "Uh, sorry. Can I help you with that flat tire?" he asked, trying to keep his thoughts on the tire and off her curves and cleavage that seemed to have vapor locked his brain. Then it sunk in that she had called him soldier. "How did you know I was military?"

"You just have that look about you. What branch?" she asked, her gaze locked with his as she waited for him to answer.

"I was a Marine, so I'd appreciate if you didn't call me soldier."

"Oh, I didn't know there was a difference. Thank you for your service. Now, my jack seems to be missing. Do you have one I can use?"

"I've got one in my truck. Why don't you find some shade, and I'll get that tire changed for you," he said, looking her up and down again. He gave himself a mental head slap to quit ogling her or she was going to think he was a total perv.

She stepped around to the side of the car, and he had to remind himself to quit staring. Her cutoff shorts showed off the length of her legs, and he had to quickly turn and head to his truck for the jack before she saw the obvious effect she was having on him. He acted as if he were digging around in his truck to try and get rid of the wood he was sporting. His jeans weren't loose enough to hide it.

After getting his libido under control, he grabbed the jack and the lug wrench and walked back to her car. He could feel her watching as he bent over to place the jack under the axle, his knee sending him a reminder of the injury he'd sustained a couple of days previously. Ignoring the pain, he flexed his muscles as he loosened the lug nuts. Might as well give her a show.

"So, what brings you to Indiana?" he asked, turning to look at her when she didn't answer right away.

She blushed at being caught staring at him as he worked. "Woodview is my hometown."

He grinned as he heaved the spare tire out, giving his muscles a little extra flex now that he knew she was watching. "Are you back to stay?" he asked, moving the tire into position and tightening the lug nuts, hoping she would say yes.

"Yeah."

He pulled a rag out of his pocket and wiped off his hands, giving her time to elaborate. When she didn't continue, he looked up and noticed the resignation in her eyes before she could hide it. He wondered what had driven her back to Woodview where she obviously didn't want to be.

"You're all set," he said before he turned and walked back toward his truck, hoping she would stop him. He looked back when he heard her car door close. She pulled away without even a glance back at him. He settled into his truck, wondering why she didn't seem happy to be home.

With a shake of his head he turned the truck around and continued his journey into town, his thoughts on the hurt and fear in her eyes, wanting to make it go away. His hands itched to feel her curves as he imagined her hair would smell like wildflowers and sunshine.

After a stop at the hardware store for paint, rollers, and brushes, he stood with his hand on the door handle and stared at the sign for the jewelry store, something telling him he needed to go inside. "No, can't be. That was just a story, wasn't it?"

They'd just returned to the house after their birthday dinner at their favorite restaurant. He'd wondered what it would be like to have a birthday all to himself. Being twins, everything was celebrated together with his brother AJ. Not

3

that he didn't love his brother. They were two pieces of one whole.

Their father sat on the porch steps, motioning for them to join him. "You're fourteen now, and it's time we talked about what it means to be a Monroe." Pulling his wallet out of his pocket, he opened it and removed a picture. "This is a picture of your mother and I when we first met. The first time I saw her, I knew she was the one for me. The Monroe men fall fast, they fall hard, and they fall forever. You'll know when you've met your forever girl.

His forever girl. How could it be her? He didn't even know her name.

Ten minutes later, he walked out of the store with a ring box in his pocket. It wasn't the biggest ring in the store, but to him, it had sparkled the brightest, drawing his attention. "Holy shit. She's the one."

Dori pulled into Rina's driveway, lost in thought about her encounter with the sexy marine. She was attracted to him, but it was too soon. It had only been a couple of days since she left her boyfriend, Ty. She shuddered at the memory of his hands on her the last time they fought and rubbed the bruise on the inside of her wrist. Luckily, a friend of his had stopped by, and she had been able to slip away. Looking up, she spied the graffiti on the barn. "What the hell?" she said, slamming the car door. "Rina?" she yelled, hoping her friend was okay.

Rina walked out of the barn with Petey close on her heels. The dog ran to Dori, jumping up until she crouched down and gave him some scratches.

"Hi, Petey! How you doing?" she asked, looking up when she heard Rina approaching. She stood and gave Rina a hug, frowning at how thin she seemed. "Hey, girl. Surprise!"

4

"What are you doing here?" Rina asked. "Did Ty come with you?"

"No. I left him. I didn't know where else to go, so I hopped in the car and headed here."

Dori looked up when she heard the screech of the screen door, ready to run if Ty had made it here before her. She looked at AJ quizzically. "How did you get here before me? You were headed the other direction." She looked at him closer and blushed. "Wait. You're not him."

"Him who?" AJ asked with a grin.

"Someone who looks an awful lot like you stopped and changed my flat tire for me."

"That was my brother, Jessie. I'm impressed you can tell us apart. Most people can't."

She wondered why other people couldn't tell them apart. To her, they didn't look alike much at all.

Rina spoke up. "This is my friend Dori. Dori, this is AJ. His brother, Jessie, lives over in the Winter's place." Jealousy blossomed in her chest at the way AJ seemed to be looking at Dori. "Jessie and AJ have been helping me out with the shelter." She turned her attention to AJ. "Dori and I went to high school together. She ran off with her boyfriend after graduation."

Dori took advantage of the lull in the conversation. "I've been on the road for hours and really need to use the restroom. I'll be right back," she said as she ran into the house.

She was washing her hands when she heard the yelling.

"AJ? Where the hell are you?"

A piece of sandpaper in his hand, AJ stomped out of the other room, pulling down his dust mask. "What? I'm trying to get the drywall done in here," he growled.

She closed the door and leaned back against it, her heart

rate increasing as she gasped for breath. "It's okay. They won't hurt me," she repeated over and over as she slid down until she was sitting on the floor, her arms wrapped around her knees. She squeezed her eyes shut and willed her heartrate to return to normal as she counted the seconds as she tried to breathe normally.

Stifling a yawn, Jessie pulled the truck up to the barn, frowning at the graffiti painted on the wall. Why would someone want to do that to Rina? They needed to figure out who was trying to drive her off her grandfather's farm. He would be defending her even if she wasn't his best friend in Woodview.

Wondering where everyone had gotten to, he walked around the house to find Rina sitting on the porch steps. She wiped at her cheeks before she looked up at him. He knew his twin had done something to make her cry.

"Where's AJ?" he asked. "You've been crying. What did he do? Do you want me to go beat him up for you?" It upset him to see her cry, especially over his thick-headed brother.

She smiled at his cavalier words. "It's nothing like that. I just gave AJ the perfect opportunity to kiss me, and he walked away again. I don't understand your brother at all."

She stomped over to the truck and grabbed a couple of paint cans and swung them out of the back of the vehicle. "Let's get started with the paint. I really don't want to look at the graffiti any longer."

"Go ahead and get started. I need to talk to AJ for a minute." He walked up the porch steps. "Sounds like I need to pound some sense into him," he muttered to himself as he reached for the screen door. "AJ? Where the hell are you?"

A piece of sandpaper in his hand, AJ stomped out of the other room, pulling down his dust mask. "What? I'm trying to get the drywall done in here," he growled.

"What's got your panties in a twist?" Jessie asked. "I want to talk to you about Rina." He sat on the sheet-covered sofa and threw his keys on the end table. "I thought I told you that Rina and I are not together. She told me she's been trying to let you know she's interested, but you keep ignoring her." Why was his brother so oblivious to Rina?

"Yes, you did tell me. But did you tell her?" he inquired.

"Why do you keep asking me that? I told you I think of her as a little sister."

AJ paced the length of the room before turning back.

"Would you just tell me why you're making such a big deal about it?"

"I'll tell you why," AJ said through gritted teeth. "Because she loves you. There, I said it. You happy now?" he snarled. "I'm sure she's only acting interested in me to make you jealous or something."

AJ walked over to the window and stared out at Rina spreading primer over the graffiti on the barn. "She said she loves you. That first day, she looked up at me and said, 'Love you, Jessie.'"

"She's said that to me, too, but she added that she loves me like a brother." Jessie still didn't understand why this was bothering AJ so much. The only time they had an issue with a girl was the whole Sasha situation. "You know I don't love her as anything other than a friend. Why is this bugging you?"

AJ looked over at Jessie. "Do you realize how many girls propositioned me in high school? There were a lot, and they all wanted you and settled for me, the 'not as cool' brother.

They all eventually admitted they were only with me to get closer to you or that they were pretending I was you." AJ grabbed Jessie's keys off the end table and strode out the door without a word. He jumped in Jessie's truck and took off.

The yelling stopped, and then she heard a door slam. Pulling herself up off the floor, she opened the door and peeked out into the hallway.

"Hey, Beauty. What are you doing here?"

Startled by his voice, she put her arms up over her head to protect her face. "Geez, you scared me." She rushed out of the room.

Dismayed by her reaction, he followed her into the kitchen and watched as she pulled a bottle of water out of the fridge. She looked at him and waved the water bottle in her hand. Grabbing one for him at his nod, she handed it to him before walking out to the front porch.

"Why did you react like you were expecting me to hit you," he asked, wanting to punch someone for making her afraid. He remembered her saying she was moving back, but she only had one suitcase in the car with her. "Who are you running from?"

"My ex-boyfriend," she said with a frown. "I don't know why I came here. This is the first place he'll look for me." She wrapped her arms around herself as if to hold herself together. "Coming here was a stupid idea." She sobbed.

He reached out and put his hand on her shoulder to show he understood what it was like to run from your demons, whether they're memories or people. Turning to face him, she wrapped her arms around him and let her tears flow.

"Well, hell," he murmured, holding her closely. "It's okay, Beauty. I won't let anything happen to you." He didn't even know her name, but he would lay down his life for her without hesitating. The thought of someone putting their hands on her made him clench his hands into fists in preparation for beating someone bloody. It was his duty to protect those weaker than himself, but this was beyond his duty; this was his heart telling him to protect her at all costs. She was his forever, and as such was precious to him.

Her sobs tapered off, and her breathing evened out. She lifted her head and looked at him, brushing at the wet spots on his shirt from her tears. "Thanks," she said. "I'm sorry about your shirt." A smile pulled at her tear-stained lips. "I do have a name, you know."

"You do?" He smirked. "I haven't heard it yet."

"You must think I'm a complete ditz." She brushed the tears off her face. "My name is Dori Graham."

He gently wiped away a tear she missed from under her eye. "I don't think that, Dori. You just had more important things on your mind," he replied before kissing her on the forehead. With a grimace, he limped down the steps, his knee sending waves of pain up his leg.

"Why are you limping?"

"That's a story for another time. Let's just say it's the reason I'm not a marine anymore and leave it at that for now." He didn't like talking about his time in Afghanistan where he watched good men die from horrible wounds. "Rina is probably wondering where you are by now." He held his hand out to help her navigate the stairs and gave her a hug before walking off toward the barn where the paint was waiting for him.

With a thumbs up to Rina, Jessie poured paint and set up the ladder to start at the top of the barn. He whistled as he rolled paint onto the barn, obliterating the graffiti. There was something satisfying about covering something so ugly with clean, white paint.

Dori sauntered over and grabbed a roller and took up a position next to Rina and started painting.

Rina leaned closer to Jessie and examined the area he'd just finished painting. "Hey, you missed a spot."

He looked down at Rina and smirked. "Nope, you need to get your eyes checked. This paint job is perfect." With a flick of his wrist, he splattered paint on the top of her head.

"Wha… Jessie, I'll get you for that."

"Big talk coming from you, little girl." He laughed as she flipped him the bird.

The slam of the door of his truck pulled his attention from his banter with Rina. He watched his brother stalking toward her with a look of determination. Finally, maybe now those two would quit dancing around each other and admit there was an attraction.

AJ took the roller out of Rina's hand and dropped it into the paint tray. Grabbing her hand, he pulled her around to the back of the barn.

With a frown, Dori dropped her roller and turned as if to follow them around the corner.

"Don't worry. He's not going to hurt her. He's just going to straighten out a little misunderstanding between the two of them. Just give them some privacy."

"Okay. But if he hurts her…"

"He won't."

He grinned when Rina stumbled back around to the front of the building and picked up the roller she'd been using and stood there staring at it.

"Rina? You trying to paint the wall telepathically?" Jessie asked with a grin. "Looks like my brother does know what to do with a woman," he said to Dori with a laugh. He continued to paint, whistling happily. When he spied AJ looking just as shell-shocked as Rina, he laughed again, glad he wasn't the one walking around like a zombie. "Better you than me, Bro," he muttered to himself as he rolled more paint onto the wall in front of him, ignoring the feelings that Dori had awakened in him and the jeweler's box hidden in his truck.

Chapter Two

THE FRAGMENTS of the dream exploded when he opened his eyes, a scream lodged in his throat. Sitting on the edge of the bed, the phantom smell of blood turned his stomach as he gulped in air, his head in his hands.

"Jessie? You okay?" Rina asked through the door.

Damn. Did he yell in his sleep? His first attempt at an answer came out as a croak. After a cough to clear his throat he replied, "Yeah. Is breakfast ready?"

"I'm ready to put the eggs on."

"Okay, give me ten minutes." Wearing only his boxers, he stumbled to the master bath, picking his sweats and t-shirt off the floor on his way. Staring into the mirror, he frowned at his blood-shot eyes and stubble-covered face. If he didn't get some uninterrupted sleep soon, AJ was going to be all up in his business.

He strolled into the kitchen, grateful that Rina had her back to him as he poured coffee into a mug. She knew him well enough that she would question the bags under his eyes. Damn. A camping trip at the nearby state park usually pushed the nightmares away for at least a couple of months, but the alone time hadn't worked this time. The nightmares were back after a couple of days. Was it due to his trip being cut short? Was the pain of wrenching his knee the culprit or was it because his brother was hovering over him?

He stood in the doorway and watched as she flipped bacon and cracked eggs into a skillet. The slight hesitation in her step as she moved to pull plates out of the cupboard reminded him that she had almost died from an infection and he hadn't noticed her illness. His only thought had been to get away.

She turned and narrowed her eyes at him, and he braced himself for the questions he saw in her eyes. He smiled at how her whole demeanor changed. Her face softened and her eyes brightened when his brother walked into the room. *Would Dori ever look at him like that?* He watched as she ducked her head and turned back to the stove and turned off the burner. "Eggs are ready. Who's hungry?"

Seeing her attention return to him, he scooped his eggs onto the toast on his plate and folded it over as he stood. "I gotta run. Don't want to be late for my shift. I'll talk to you later." Stopping only to kiss the top of her head, he hurried out of the room.

Shoving the last bite of his makeshift sandwich into his mouth, he picked up his work bag and threw it onto the seat of his truck before he took off, worry about the nightmare fighting memories of Dori's smile for his attention.

The ambulance was not in its spot when he pulled into the fire station. Thank God for small favors. He had time to get his head together before he had to start his shift. He opened the center console and pulled out a ring box. As if in a daze, he'd stopped and bought an engagement ring on his way into town to pick up the painting supplies the day before. The Monroe insta-love had struck him as he stared at the curvaceous blonde as he changed her flat tire. He'd scoffed at the idea until it took hold of his brain and his heart. Resisting it was as impossible as not breathing. He couldn't believe it when he'd walked out of the store with the ring box in his hand, his mind whirling with the knowledge he would marry her, but he hadn't even known her name.

Lost in his memories, he didn't notice his fellow EMT, Cam, pull into the lot and park beside him. At the tapping on his window, he shoved the ring box back into the compartment and slammed it shut.

Grabbing his bag, he exited his vehicle, his knee protesting at the sudden movement. "Hey, Cam."

"I didn't think you would be in today with your knee. You up for a full shift today?"

"I'm fine," he snapped as he limped into the station. "A couple of aspirin and I'll be good as new."

"Good. Glad to have you back. Now, you going to tell me who the ring is for?"

"Ring? What ring?" Crap. He hadn't gotten the ring out of sight quickly enough.

"I thought I was your best friend. Who've you been seeing, and how have you kept it a secret?"

Rummaging around in his bag for the aspirin bottle, he wondered how to explain his feelings for Dori to Cam without sounding like a lunatic. Washing down a couple of the pills with a drink from his water bottle, he turned to face his friend. "I'm not even sure I believe it myself, but I met the one."

"When? And why didn't you tell me?"

He slammed his locker closed as he mumbled, "I just met her yesterday."

"Yesterday?" Cam glared at Jessie. "What, did she cast a

spell on you or something? Nobody meets someone and buys a ring the next day. Are you nuts?"

"I just might be. And just to set the record straight, I bought the ring yesterday."

"Holy shit, Jess. You are nuts. How much is she paying you? That's the only reason I can think of that you bought an engagement ring for someone the same day you met them."

"Nope. No money exchanged hands. It's a Monroe thing, knowing when we've met the one. I didn't believe it either until it happened. Hopefully, she'll feel the same eventually."

"Well, better you than me. I'm not ready to settle down yet."

"What about Mary? Haven't you been seeing her for a while now?"

"I love her and all, but…"

"You can't keep playing the field forever, Cam."

"Mary understands and is okay with the way things are. Maybe someday I'll be ready to make the leap but not any time soon."

"Someday will come sooner than you think."

After feeding and watering the dogs, Dori and Rina walked to Rina's car parked next to the house. As they closed the car doors, AJ walked out of the house and jogged to the car.

"Dogs all taken care of?" he asked Rina through the open window. At her nod, he continued, "Call me when you get to Jessie's. I'll see you at dinner." Poking his head into the car, he kissed her and then sauntered back into the house.

Rina blushed as she put the car in drive and drove off.

Once they reached Jessie's house, Rina pulled Dori back to the bedroom she'd been using. "We need to talk. I saw your expression when AJ kissed me. What happened with Ty, and why does affection scare you?"

"I don't want to talk about it. What about you and AJ? Do you think he's the one?" Dori waited for Rina to answer, wishing she could be so carefree when AJ's brother was close to her. How could he affect her so deeply when she hardly knew him?

"I do. When I look at AJ, I can't imagine my life without him in it."

"Surely it's not that simple. Look at what happened the last time I followed my heart." She waited for the inevitable questions from her friend.

Rina turned to face her. "How did it start? When you two left town, you seemed to have the perfect relationship." When Dori's eyes filled with tears, she pulled her toward the bed and motioned for her to sit.

"I don't know how it happened. One day, everything was great and then poof. It was as if Ty was replaced by an asshole who looked just like him. I really don't want to talk about this right now." Trying to direct the conversation to a different topic she asked, "What do you want to cook for dinner?" Her attention on her phone, she looked up when Rina's phone dinged with a text notification. "That was AJ, wasn't it?" Dori asked, noticing the silly grin spread across Rina's face from her spot on the bed.

"Yeah. We're going out to dinner. Oh God. What am I going to wear?" Frantic, she rummaged through the clothes in the closet, grimacing at the lack of choices. "I'm going to have to go home and get something. I don't have anything here that will work." She picked up her purse and pulled Dori with her toward the door. "Come on. You've got to help me find something."

Dori stopped. "Slow down. Your closet isn't going anywhere. I just need to grab my phone."

Dori jumped when Jessie knocked on the doorframe. Geez, she needed to get her reactions under control or he would want to know why she was so jumpy.

"What do you want for dinner tonight? I could go pick up Chinese."

"None for me." Rina replied with a grin. "I have a date. See ya later, Jessie!" she yelled over her shoulder as she sprinted out of the house with Dori right behind her.

Dori turned and yelled back to Jessie. "Chinese sounds great! I'll text you…" Rina pulled her out the door to the sound of Jessie's laughter.

Instead of taking Dori's car, they walked the trail that would take them to Rina's house.

"I'm glad you found someone, Rina. AJ is totally in love with you."

"Yeah, he's pretty great."

"I know he seems great right now, but if that ever changes, you let me know. No way do I want you to go through what I did."

Rina put her arm around Dori's shoulders and pulled her close. "Don't you worry. AJ isn't like that."

"I know, but I want you to promise you'll tell me if he ever touches you in anger."

"Okay. I promise."

AJ met them at the door when they arrived at Rina's, pulling Rina off toward the dining room.

Wanting to give them some time alone, Dori trudged up the stairs, happy her friend had found someone who loved her. After texting Jessie her preferences for dinner, she pulled open the closet door and rummaged through the clothes hanging on the rod. Pulling out a sundress, she decided that it would be perfect for her friend's dinner date, along with a pair of sandals.

When Rina walked into the room, she grinned, a dreamy look in her eyes. "Oh, that dress will be perfect. Will you help me do my hair after I shower?"

They talked and giggled as they had done back in high school.

Checking her reflection in the full-length mirror, Rina gushed, "I feel like a princess. It's been so long since I dressed up or went out with a guy." She glanced over at the nightstand when one of their phones chirped.

Dori picked up her phone. "It was mine. Jessie's leaving for Ming's, and he's just double-checking my order." Typing in her reply, she hit send as Rina's phone chirped. She carried it over to Rina. "Is AJ ready to go? You are so lucky. You should see the way he looks at you when he thinks no one is looking." She fanned herself. "Those looks should be sending you up in flames!"

Rina smiled."Oh yeah. They are."

They heard the sound of a vehicle coming up the drive, and Rina peeked out the window. "That's him. I'll see you later at Jessie's." She walked to the stairs, turning for one last comment to her friend. "Don't forget to set the alarm when you leave."

"I won't. Have fun, and we'll talk tomorrow."

Dori gathered up the makeup they'd left lying on the counter and put it in the makeup bag. Picking up the clothes Rina wanted to take to Jessie's, she stopped to listen when she heard a board creak. *It's nothing. It's just this old house settling.* Turning to the bed, she placed the clothes in her arms into a duffel bag.

After toting the duffel down to the foyer, she remembered she'd left her phone upstairs on the dresser. When she turned to trot back up the stairs, someone grabbed her from behind, pinning her arms to her sides.

"Stop struggling. I don't want to hurt you," a gravelly voice said into her ear. She froze, hoping it would give her a chance to get away. When she felt the intruder loosen his hold, she bolted toward the door, screaming for help. Tackled from behind and her reactions slowed by the terror washing through her, her head connected with the cast iron doorstop with a sickening thud.

Jessie pulled up into his driveway after picking up dinner, wondering why Dori hadn't picked up when he'd called while he was at Ming's. He'd gotten extra sauces since he didn't know which she preferred. After depositing the bags of food on the kitchen table, he searched the house, his worry ratcheting up when he didn't find her. Maybe her phone was turned off or needed to be charged. Telling himself not to worry, he jumped back in his truck and sped over to Rina's.

When he pulled up into Rina's drive, he tooted the horn, expecting to see an exasperated Dori come running. The dogs barked out back in the shelter but no Dori. Reaching over, he pulled his handgun out of the glove box, the gun feeling solid and comforting in his hand. The side door opened silently at his touch, his nerve endings alive with adrenaline. The lack of a beep from the alarm deepened his worry; the girls had both been reminded to set it even when they were in the house. "Hey, Beauty, where are you?" he yelled as he slowly pushed it open, remembering her reaction when he startled her earlier in the day. "Dori? You here?" Flipping on the light in the kitchen, he walked across the room and into the living room. "Dammit, Dori! Where are you?" In the back of his mind, he knew he should be calling 911, but he couldn't think of anything but finding her. His stomach rolled when he spotted the small pool of blood near the front door, forcing him to stop and remind himself to breathe. If someone hurt his Beauty...

Clearing each room as he was trained to do in the Marines, he found the downstairs was empty. Creeping up the stairs, he stopped halfway up the staircase when he heard a noise from Rina's bedroom.

Shadows hid the details of the room, giving an intruder ample hiding places. He flipped the light switch, lighting up the room and hopefully giving him a few precious seconds for him to react as the intruder's eyes adjusted to the brightness. His heart wanted to stop beating when he discovered Dori tied up and lying on the floor on the other side of the bed. Ignoring the pain, he dropped to his knees and reached out to brush the blood-matted hair off her face. His heart thumped painfully until she opened her eyes and looked up at him. "Don't move, Beauty. I'm here." The fear in her eyes tested his tenuous grip on his temper. "This may hurt a bit," he commented before he removed the duct tape covering her mouth.

Pulling his pocketknife from his pocket, he cut the rope from around her wrists and ankles, checking for other injuries. Satisfied the cut on her forehead was the only injury, he dialed 911 to report the break-in and request an ambulance, mentioning to the dispatcher they were upstairs in the front bedroom.

"Are you sure he's gone?" Dori tried to sit up to look past the bed.

"I checked the house. Whoever did this is not here now. Lie back and let me see to that cut." He pulled the comforter off the bed and covered her, wanting to keep her from going into shock from the experience.

Moving to stand, he stopped when she grabbed his hand.

"Don't leave me," she whispered, the fear in her eyes different than what he saw earlier.

"I'm not going anywhere," he assured her. "I just want to get the first aid kit so I can get this head wound cleaned up a little."

"No, stay, please," she implored, looking around the room. "He might come back."

"Okay. As long as you lie still." Watching for any sign of concussion, he held her hand and rubbed his thumb across her soft skin.

"What do you remember? Did you see his face?"

"I had just brought the bag of Rina's clothes down to take over to your place when I remembered I left my phone upstairs. When I turned back to the stairs, he grabbed me from behind, pinning my arms to my sides. I froze. I don't think he expected that. His hold loosened enough that I got away and started running." She shivered, the memory of the intruder's hands on her reminding her of Ty.

One-handed, he tucked the comforter closer to her.

"He tackled me from behind, and that's the last thing I remember until I woke up here. He told me this was my last warning as if I should know what this was all about. He must have thought I was Rina. You need to tell her. She needs to be careful. This guy might come back.

A siren screamed in the distance, getting louder as it approached the house.

"Finally," he said as he stood.

"Jessie?"

"Up here, Cam!" he yelled, glad it was his friend.

Cam walked in pulling the gurney, his partner following, looking confused when he didn't see Jessie.

"Over here, Cam," Jessie called. "Beside the bed."

Dori relaxed when she saw Cam. "Hey, Cam."

"Dori? When did you get back?" he asked as he started cleaning up her head wound, frowning at the blood matted in her hair. "You're going to need some stitches. Looks like you're going for an ambulance ride." They helped her get settled on the gurney. "You riding along, Jess?"

"No. I need to check on the dogs, and then I'll meet you there." He turned and grabbed Dori's hand. "I'll be there as soon as I can, Beauty." He kissed her fingers, ignoring the look of astonishment from Cam. "Watch out for her, Cam. This really shook her up. I'll talk to you at the hospital."

After Dori was loaded into the ambulance, Jessie headed for the barn with a deputy. Relieved to find everything locked up tight, he still checked on the dogs to be sure they were all okay. Once his mind was at ease about the animals, he finished up with the deputy and rushed to his truck. Seated in his truck, he ran his fingers through his hair, dreading he had to ruin AJ and Rina's date. The adrenaline from finding Dori had worn off, and his hands shook as he selected AJ's cell number. The memory of Dori lying on the floor, her face covered in blood, made him feel sick. He had just met her, but the intensity of his feelings was not a surprise. The Monroe men fell fast, they fell hard, and they fell forever. That would teach him to make fun of how AJ acted around Rina. He would probably be doing the same things around Dori.

After talking with AJ and reassuring him that Dori would be okay, Jessie drove to the hospital. Walking into the emergency department, he stopped and asked the receptionist what treatment room Dori was in. The hallway was crowded with doctors and nurses hurrying about their business. "Hey, Cam. Which doctor is on tonight?"

"Fairfield is on tonight. She's in good hands." Cam pulled some supplies off of a shelf. "Dori's the one you bought the ring for, isn't she?" At Jessie's nod, he continued asking questions. "What happened? How did she get upstairs? I saw the blood pool down by the door."

Jessie explained about the incidents out at Rina's. "I think it's been going on for a while. I plan on getting some answers from Rina." He absently rubbed his leg at the twinge of pain. "Be on the lookout for anything out of the ordinary around here."

"I may be able to shed some light on what's happening." Cam's radio crackled, and a voice came over, calling the ambulance to a car accident out on the highway. "Gotta run. I'll stop and talk to you tomorrow."

Jessie watched Cam hurry away, wondering what he knew. His mind whirling with questions, he poked his head into the treatment room. "Hey, Doc F., how's my girl doing?" he asked, noting that the doctor hadn't started stitching yet.

Dori looked over and smiled at him, making his heart skip a beat. "I'm glad you made it, Marine. I hate needles. Please take my mind off of this."

Pulling the visitor's chair closer, he sat and took her hand. "No worries. I'm here now, Beauty."

She leaned back and let the doctor start the stitches, holding tight to Jessie's hand.

Jessie and the doctor walked out of the room to find AJ and Rina waiting anxiously.

"Is she okay?" Rina asked. She looked like she would shatter into a million pieces any minute.

"Hey. She's okay. Just a few stitches and she'll be as good as new," Jessie told her as he pulled her into a hug. He set her away from him, placing his hands on her shoulders. "Her attacker thought she was you. I know you're not telling us everything about the problems you've been having with break-ins at the shelter and why you can't access your money.

We will talk about this tomorrow, and you will tell us the truth. It's affecting other people now." He tried to keep the anger out of his voice, but finding Dori tied up and bleeding had shaken him up more than he wanted to admit.

"This is all my fault. I didn't think anyone else would get hurt."

AJ pulled her out of Jessie's hands, frowning at her tears. "We'll make sure everyone is safe, Rina. Everything will be okay. I promise." He looked over at Jessie. "You make sure the girls are safe tonight. I'll make sure the dogs are okay. Between the two of us, we should be able to keep an eye on everything."

Jessie walked back into the treatment room, followed by AJ and Rina.

Rina rushed over to Dori. "I'm so sorry! This is all my fault."

"No, it's not. I forgot to set the alarm after you left. It was like an open invitation for the guy to just come on in. He probably wouldn't have hurt me if I hadn't tried to get away." She reached up and felt the dried blood caked in her hair. "Ugh! Can you help me wash my hair tonight? This is gross."

"Sure. I'll get you fixed up." Rina looked up when the nurse walked in with Dori's discharge paperwork. "Do you want me to call your dad?" she asked.

"No!" Dori replied heatedly. "I don't want to talk to him. Don't you call him…" She stopped when she realized the nurse was staring at her.

"Here's your discharge paperwork and wound care instructions."

Two hours later, the girls were parked on the couch, flipping through channels to find something they wanted to watch. Jessie strolled over with a bowl of popcorn and a glass of wine, handing both to Rina.

Dori looked up at him. "Hey, where's mine?"

"No alcohol for you tonight. Ladies on pain meds don't get to drink," he said with a grin as AJ walked in and handed her a soda. "You'll just have to deal with it. I'll take you out for drinks when you're done with the painkillers."

"You are no fun," she said continuing the banter. "I guess if you're going to be the alcohol police, I'll have to be a good girl tonight."

They settled on a chick flick, eliciting groans from both AJ and Jessie. Jessie sat next to Dori with his arm around her. About halfway through the movie, Jessie noticed that both Rina and Dori had fallen asleep. AJ stood, moving slowly to avoid waking Rina. He picked her up and carried her into the guest bedroom.

AJ walked out of the bedroom. "I guess I better get going and check on the dogs. I think we should have someone at Rina's twenty-four seven after what happened today."

Jessie nodded. "I agree. My next shift isn't until next week. I hope we can get this cleared up by then."

AJ called his dog, Gunner, and walked to the door. "I'll let you know if anything happens. Be safe, Bro."

"You, too."

Once his brother had closed the door, Jessie turned and watched Dori as she slept. He brushed the hair off of her face, thankful that she wasn't hurt worse by the intruder.

Flinching at his touch, Dori opened her eyes and looked up at him with a smile. "Hey, Jessie. I must have fallen asleep." She sat up straighter before pushing herself up off the couch. "Thanks for finding me today. I'm glad it was you," she said as she ran her hand down his face before turning and walking into the bedroom.

"Goodnight, Beauty," he whispered to himself as he turned off the lights and the television.

25

Chapter Three

ONCE EVERYONE HAD BEEN UPDATED on the events leading up to Dori being attacked, Cam left to meet his girlfriend, and Rina and AJ had gone to another room in the house.

Jessie watched as Dori grabbed the bread off the counter and then rummaged in the refrigerator for lunch meat and condiments. She started making sandwiches for everyone, sniffling, obviously trying to keep the tears from falling. He walked over and put his hand on her shoulder and turned her around to face him. He scowled when she stiffened up at his touch.

"Come here, Beauty," he said. He pulled her into his arms and tucked her head under his chin. He held her closely, wanting to get his hands on whoever made her afraid to be touched.

She looked up when they heard the door open. AJ walked in, his shoulders slumped and his eyes downcast as he pulled a bottle of water out of the fridge. Without a word, he shuffled out of the kitchen.

"You okay now, Beauty?" Jessie asked.

At her nod, he let her go and followed AJ out of the room.

Jessie found AJ in Rina's temporary room, sitting on the bed, his inhaler in his hand. "You okay, Bobo?" He walked in and sat on the bed next to him. He could hear AJ wheezing. He looked at him. "I thought you were done with the asthma."

AJ used the inhaler again. Jessie waited as his brother took a slow, deep breath, noting the wheezing had lessened.

"It only flares up when I let myself get too stressed. I usually only use an inhaler once every couple of weeks, but worrying about Rina has got me tied up in knots." He stood and started pacing. "I don't know how she ended up being so important to me in such a short time." He stood at the window with his hands in his pockets, staring out at the sky. "It's as if finding her out cold on your porch turned on this protective feeling. I've felt it before but never this intensely. And then she looks at me with those eyes…" He ran his hands through his hair, trying to stop their shaking. "I think I fell in love with her in that moment."

"I understand, Bobo," Jessie said. "When I stopped to change Dori's flat tire, it felt like I found something that was missing, the other half of my heart." He looked over at AJ who had turned to face him. "The first time I saw her, I was a goner. Every time she flinches when I touch her, it makes me want to punch someone. Someone treated her badly, and I really want to rearrange his face."

"Glad to know it's not just me. It's a Monroe thing, this falling in love at first sight," AJ said with a smile. "Remember Dad telling us how he fell in love with Mom the first time he saw her at that dance? After that first glance, there was no one else for him, not even after she died."

"Remember how Dad could always make her giggle like a schoolgirl? Her love for him shone in her eyes for the world

27

to see." Jessie smiled. "I never believed him when he told us about that night they met, but now I do. I have this connection with Dori that I can't explain." He turned and reached into his pocket. "I bought this yesterday after I met her." He showed AJ the engagement ring. "I know she is the one. It's hard to believe I just met her yesterday."

AJ grinned. "Congrats, Jess! I guess it runs in the family," he said with a laugh. He opened his hand and showed Jessie the ring he'd bought for Rina after their kiss behind the barn. "How did we both meet the girl for us in the same week? It's got to be a twin thing."

Rina looked up from the cutting board where she was slicing tomatoes for the sandwiches when AJ and Jessie walked into the kitchen. "Where did you two disappear to?" she asked as she continued slicing.

AJ took the knife out of her hand and laid it on the cutting board next to the tomato. "We were talking about the two girls we met recently and how they make us feel." He sat in one of the chairs around the kitchen table, pulling her down into his lap. "I was going to wait for the perfect time, but I can't think of a better time to do this than with my brother here."

He dug around in his pocket, pulling the ring out, keeping it hidden from Rina. "I have a question I want to ask you. I know we've only known each other a little over a week, but I just can't wait any longer." He stood and sat Rina on the chair as he bent down onto one knee. "The first moment I saw you, my heart felt like it had come home. Will you marry me, Rina?" He watched her face, hoping he wouldn't see horror at his question.

Rina looked down at the ring in AJ's hand, hiding her shocked expression behind the hair hanging in her face. She looked up and smiled at the uncertainty in AJ's face. "Yes, I will."

At her nod, he stood and scooped her up into his arms. "Thank God," he whispered. He lowered his lips to hers and kissed her with everything in his heart.

Dori and Jessie turned and tiptoed out of the kitchen, letting them have some time alone.

Dori looked up at Jessie. "They just met this week? Wow, that's fast but so romantic." She turned and walked toward the bedrooms, hoping that Jessie didn't hear the wistfulness in her voice. "They'll probably be all lovey-dovey now," she muttered, trying to keep the envy and jealousy hidden. She jumped when she felt a hand drop onto her shoulder, relaxing when she realized it was Jessie.

"You're jealous!" he crowed, hoping against hope that he was right. "You girls all seem to love romantic gestures." He grinned as the ring seemed to burn a hole in his pocket. As much as he wanted to whip it out and ask her right now, he knew it wasn't the right time. "I've got an idea. Want to help?" He grabbed her hand and pulled her to the front door. "Let's go!"

Fifteen minutes later, they returned to Jessie's house.

Rina noticed the guitar case. "What's that for? Do you play?"

Jessie just grinned as he opened the case and pulled out the guitar.

AJ smiled. "That's where you disappeared to for so long. I wondered where you two were."

"I made a promise to Mom and Dad that if you ever got engaged, I would sing this song for you and your fiancée."

The strings vibrated with sound as he strummed the first chord. AJ's eyes shone with unshed tears, testament to how much he was moved by this simple act.

AJ pulled Rina to her feet and into his arms, holding her close and swaying to the music as Dori added her voice to Jessie's. By the end of the song, everyone was trying to hide the intense effect the song had on them.

AJ looked down at Rina. "I know it was quick, but I just couldn't wait. The Monroe men fall fast, and they fall forever."

They all sat around the table as Jessie and AJ reminisced about their parents and the love they shared. Rina and Dori both sighed, loving the story of love at first sight and marriage at nineteen that lasted until their last breath.

After a couple of hours, both AJ and Jessie realized that no one had been watching the shelter for most of the afternoon.

"We better get over there," AJ remarked as he helped clean up the dishes from lunch. "I hope nothing happened while we were here celebrating." He smiled looking over at Rina wiping off the table. "I am such a lucky guy."

Jessie put the last plate in the cupboard before he turned to AJ. "You ready to go? The girls can come over later. I'm sure they want to spend some time giggling over that ring."

At AJ's nod, Jessie walked over to Dori and let her know they were headed to Rina's.

She looked up into his eyes, seeming to like what she found there. "We'll be over later. We need to start discussing the wedding."

"Already? They haven't even set a date yet." Jessie grinned. "What is it with girls and weddings?"

Dori punched him in the arm. "That's enough out of you. Go take care of the dogs." She reached up and pulled him down to her for a quick kiss before she pushed him toward the door. "And take your brother with you!" she said as she spied AJ and Rina in a lip-lock.

Jessie grabbed AJ and pulled him away from Rina. "Come on, Romeo. We've got a job to do now. There will be time for that later." He pulled his brother out the door, laughing at his dazed expression. "You are such a goner."

"Just wait and see how you feel when Dori has your ring on her finger. The feeling is incredible." They strolled toward the barn, grinning like a couple of idiots.

The knocking on the door pulled him from the nightmare filled with blood and sand and despair. "Jessie? You okay?" His mood improved slightly just hearing his Beauty's voice.

"Yeah," he answered. Shoving the memory of the dream out of his head, he stepped into the shower, shivering when the cold water hit his skin. The shock of the cold woke him up fully and focused his mind on the task at hand: keep the girls safe and find out who was behind Rina's problems.

"Morning, Beauty," he said as he poured coffee into his mug. "What's on the agenda for today?"

"I need to start looking for a job and, eventually, an apartment. I can't stay here forever."

"That's not a good idea. At least wait until we catch whoever it was that attacked you yesterday."

"I won't be treated like a prisoner. I came here to… Oh, never mind." Her coffee cup hit the table with a thump before she scurried out of the kitchen. He heard a door slam and hoped it was the bedroom door. She didn't need to be outside where she was a target.

Rina sauntered into the room, stifling a yawn with her hand. "What did you say to Dori? She blew past me like a whirlwind, and she didn't look happy."

"Was she headed for the bedroom or outside?" he asked as he set his mug in the sink.

"She picked up my jacket off the chair, so I think she was headed outside."

"Well, shit. You stay in the house until I get back."

The front door opened, and Jessie hurried out of the kitchen, hoping it was Dori coming back inside.

"Hey, Jess, what's wrong?" AJ asked after seeing the expression on his brother's face.

"Dori took off. When I mentioned her staying here until we caught the person responsible for her attack, she got mad and stormed out. I have to go find her."

"I didn't see her on the road, so she must have taken the path over to Rina's." He handed the leash in his hand to his brother. "Take Gunner with you. He'd enjoy a nice long walk."

"Thanks, Bobo. I'll be back."

Jessie stomped down the trail, fuming and muttering about willful women. His knee ached from the exertion as he hurried toward Dori. Gunner yipped when they walked into the clearing behind Rina's house, pulling Jessie toward the animal shelter in the barn. "Want to visit the inmates, do ya? Let's go then."

The door was propped open to let in the breeze and air out the kennel area. He could hear kennel doors rattling and the happy barks of the dogs. He walked through the reception area and poked his head through the door to the back rooms. "Dori, you back here?"

"Shit."

He walked into the kennel area and found her seated on the floor with a small dog in her arms. Gunner strained his leash, wanting to get closer to her.

Unclipping the leash from the dog's collar, he let AJ's dog run over and start licking her face.

"Hey, Gunner. Yes, I missed you too. Now, you lie

down." The dog complied, putting his head down on his front paws.

"You're good with the dogs."

"I used to be a certified trainer, but I had to give it up." She buried her face in the small dog's fur.

"Hey, why the tears? No one's keeping you from working with the dogs. We just want to be sure you're safe."

"That's what he used to say."

"He who?"

"Never mind," she stated as she stood. She placed the dog back in its kennel and closed the door.

"I just want to be free to do what I want. Is that too much to ask?"

"Actually, yes. If anything happened to you, Rina would never forgive herself. You've become a target, so you get twenty-four-hour protection just like Rina."

"Maybe it would be better if I left town. I've probably been here too long as it is."

"Who are you running from, Dori? Let me help."

"Thanks, but no. This is something I need to deal with, and I won't drag anyone else into it."

Walking up behind her, he put his hands on her arms, frowning at her flinch. "At least let me protect you while you're here. Blame it on my military training, but I can't let you put yourself in harm's way, not while I'm around."

She turned and looked at him, using her fingers to brush the hair off his forehead. "I wish I could stay."

"Don't go. I can protect you." He pulled her into his arms and kissed the top of her head. "If you go, I'm afraid I won't ever see you again."

"Someday I'll come back."

"Why can't today be someday?"

She pulled away and walked to another kennel and

opened the door. "You're better off without me. Now, let me work with the dogs."

Returning to the reception area, he crossed the room and walked outside and stared out across the field behind the barn. Who was she running from and why? Resigned to keeping his distance for now, he sat on the bench beside the door to wait for her to finish her work with the dogs.

Chapter Four

RINA AND DORI poured a couple glasses of sweet tea and headed out on the deck, pulling two chairs over to the railing so they could look out over the fields in back of the house.

"So," Dori began, "how's it feel to be engaged? That was so romantic." She stared off into the distance, a faraway look in her eyes, dreaming of the day she would get her happily ever after. "How did you know he's the one?"

"I don't know. I just know that I would never be the same if he were no longer in my life. I can't believe I love him so much after just a few days." Rina looked down at the ring on her finger. "This all feels like a dream."

"Well, it's not a dream, so you need to start thinking about what kind of wedding you want. Large or small, indoor or outdoor ceremony, or you could just run off to Vegas and elope. If you go to Vegas, you better take me with you." She smiled at the thought of her friend marrying someone who seemed as great as AJ. That thought brought up images of Jessie and those eyes that seemed to be able to see down into her soul.

"Earth to Dori." Rina snickered. "Gee, I wonder where you went. You were thinking about Jessie, weren't you?"

Dori blushed. "How did you guess? I just want someone to love me like AJ loves you." Dori turned to Rina. "He seems to be a good guy, but I don't know if I can commit to a relationship again after all I went through with Ty."

Rina sipped her tea, trying to decide if she should ask Dori about Ty. It was obvious something bad had happened to send Dori running back to Woodview alone. "What happened with Ty?" Scooting her chair closer to Dori's, Rina questioned her further. "I can tell it was something bad. Please tell me. Maybe I can help."

"The only thing that would help would be if Ty fell off the face of the earth forever. He's an asshole, and I don't want anything to do with him."

Rina put her hand over Dori's. "Tell me more about what happened so I know how much to hate him. Seriously, you need to tell me." She brushed the hair out of Dori's eyes. "You know I won't judge."

Dori turned her face away from Rina, not wanting her to see her tears. "It started out as pinches when I did something he didn't like. After a while, it was slaps, and it gradually escalated to him using his belt on me."

"Oh, Dori. I'm so sorry. I had no idea. I never liked him for you, but I had no idea he was so controlling and abusive."

"I still don't know how it happened. I thought everything was okay, and then it all changed so quickly. He would act all lovey-dovey in public, but in private..." She looked down at her hands. "He would grin at me as he punched me, always where it wouldn't show. An overcooked roast earned me a punch to the ribs. When he found a dead leaf that had fallen off a houseplant, he punched me in the stomach. Then, he started using a belt. He knew how to leave a red mark without breaking the skin."

"Why didn't you call me? I would have come to get you." Rina grabbed a couple of napkins off the table and handed them to her friend. "I'm so sorry you had to go through that."

"I wanted to call, but he took my cell phone with him whenever he left the house. All calls and texts were also sent to his phone, so he would know if I tried to contact anyone."

"What about the police? Couldn't they help you?"

"You know how he is, making friends with everyone. He hung out at the cop bars and had them all convinced I couldn't be trusted to be out on my own. The few times he took me with him, I wasn't even allowed to go to the ladies' room on my own. Working was out of the question, and all shopping was done as a couple."

Rina stood and paced the length of the deck before turning back to look at Dori.

"I was trapped. One night, Ty got drunk and forgot to hide the keys to my car, so I snuck out and left. I had about five hundred dollars I'd been hiding from him by keeping a dollar here and there. It took me a couple of years to save it. It would have to be enough to get me away from him. After shoving some clothes in a bag, I took off, driving straight through from Los Angeles, watching my rearview mirror the whole way."

"That sounds so scary. Driving all that way alone thinking Ty would catch up with you at any moment."

"When Jessie stopped to help when I got a flat, I almost crawled into the car and locked all the doors. Somehow, I gathered the courage to let him change the tire. Something about him seemed so safe and solid." She hugged herself, remembering the feeling of being vulnerable and somehow trusting the stranger who had stopped to help.

"You like Jessie, don't you? I can see it on your face when you think no one's watching. I've known him for a year, and he's nothing like Ty. He has no need to impress anyone. He's a 'take me as I am' kind of guy. I hope you'll be able to give him a chance."

"I don't think I'm ready for anything more than friendship. He watches me, and it freaks me out even though I know he won't hurt me. When he gets close, the memories of the slaps and hits take over, and it's all I can do not to scream and run away."

Rina picked up her glass of tea and took a drink. "He can tell you're afraid. I see how he freezes when you flinch."

"He seems really nice, but I don't know if I can let myself be that open again." She wiped at her eyes and squared her shoulders. "That's enough about me. We've got a wedding to plan."

The dishes were washed and the leftovers stowed away when Dori's phone rang, startling her out of her daydream of running a dog training program. She had read an article on the need for therapy dogs for veterans returning to civilian life, and she knew that was what she wanted to do. Her mind on the paperwork she'd downloaded earlier to get certified as a therapy dog trainer, she answered her phone without looking to see who it was. "Hello?" she answered as she turned back to the sink.

"I told you I would never let you go."

"How did you get this number?"

Jessie put his hand on her shoulder. "What's wrong?"

She tensed from the touch and lost her grip on her phone, watching in horror as it plopped into the sink full of dishwater. "Oh shit!"

Jessie removed his hand and shoved it in his pocket.

"Sorry about that. I should have let you know I was behind you."

She plunged her hand into the soapy water and retrieved her phone. "Not your fault. I'm just a butterfingers today."

He walked over to the cupboard and pulled out a plastic container of rice. "Here, we can try putting it in here. The rice will absorb the water and hopefully save the phone."

"Does that really work?" Her mind whirled with the knowledge that Ty had tracked down her new cell phone number. Shit.

"Yeah. I've done it a couple of times." Removing the case, he took the back cover off and put the phone in the container. "It may take a couple of days, but the rice should do the trick."

"Thanks for the tip."

"You still jump when I touch you. You know I'd never hurt you, don't you?"

"I'm sorry I'm so jumpy."

"Why is it so hard for you to relax around me? Did I do something to hurt you?" He'd thought they'd been getting closer after she was attacked, but now she was retreating from him again.

"I can't talk about it, not with you." She picked at some dried skin around her thumbnail. "I want to be able to open up to you. Maybe soon."

Upset with her answer, he turned to walk out of the room. "I'll be here when you're ready to talk."

Chapter Five

AFTER TWO DAYS of avoiding Dori, Jessie needed something to relieve some stress. Maybe tossing bags of dog food around would burn off some of his frustration. After a few days of no incidents at the shelter, they decided it was safe for both of them to make a dog food run.

Jessie tossed the keys to his brother. "You drive."

"What's up? You usually insist on driving. In fact, you've been known to refuse to go unless you were driving. You feeling okay?"

"Yeah. Just tired." He rubbed his eyes, wishing the nightmares would stay away for just one night so he could get some real sleep.

"The nightmares are back, aren't they? You need to talk to someone about them."

Stifling a yawn, he frowned at his brother. He knew AJ was right, but he hated talking about the nightmares, which were a combination of memories and fears. "They just want to shove pills at me that don't work. I just need a few days out in the woods alone. That's always worked before."

"Well, you need to schedule some time off soon. Even Cam has mentioned it to me. He's worried about you."

"You all need to quit worrying about me. I'll be fine. Worry about whoever is harassing Rina."

Tossing the fifty pound bags of dog food into the truck helped Jessie burn off some resentment toward his brother. He knew AJ worried, but he was fine. Nothing a few days of camping wouldn't fix.

As they traveled the back roads toward Rina's, they noticed the smell of smoke, but it didn't quite smell like leaves burning. Jessie frowned, knowing some idiot burning leaves on a windy day was a bad idea. A black plume of smoke became visible as they approached Rina's.

They pulled into the drive and around the house, horrified to find the smoke coming from the back half of the barn. AJ slammed on the brakes and threw the shifter into park before jumping out and running toward the barn.

Jessie ran after him, calling 911. They ran into the reception area, yelling for Rina. The dogs were barking, making it hard for them to hear if she was answering.

AJ found her in the storage room. "Rina, thank God! The barn is on fire. You've got to get out of here!"

"On fire?" The smoke rapidly started seeping into the room. "The dogs!" She held her hand over her mouth, coughing and choking on the smoke. "We've got to get them out!" She ran toward the kennels.

Jessie grabbed her arm. "Get out, Rina! AJ and I will get the dogs."

"No! I'm not leaving them!"

Jessie led Rina toward the door and held her back when she tried to run back into the barn.

"Petey! Where's Petey?" She sobbed. "I shut him in the office when I went into the storeroom."

The smoke billowed out of every door and window.

"Rina, promise me you'll stay out here if I go back in for Petey." At her nod, he turned and ran back into the barn as they started hearing sirens.

Jessie squinted through the thick, black smoke, waving his hand in front of him in attempt to spot his brother. "AJ! The fire department is almost here. Wait for them! They have the equipment to deal with this! Rina says she locked Petey up in the office. You get out, and I'll get him."

AJ ignored him and made his way to the office.

Jessie turned to follow AJ when he heard Rina screaming for AJ. "I'm coming in there after you, AJ Monroe."

Knowing she was stubborn enough to do it despite having promised to stay outside, he ran back toward the door, pulling Rina away from the barn as the firefighters began spraying water on the roof.

AJ stumbled out of the barn, coughing and gasping for air. Rina twisted out of Jessie's grip and ran up to AJ and threw her arms around him. She pulled away and gently brushed the soot off his face. "Oh my God, AJ. Are you okay?"

AJ knelt to the ground and bent over trying to catch his breath. He let go of Petey, who scurried over to Rina. "I'm okay," AJ said in between coughing fits. "Just need some fresh air."

Jessie frowned at AJ's wheezing. "Let me be the judge of that." He led AJ over to the ambulance that just drove up. "Cam, get the oxygen. AJ just had to play the hero." He made AJ sit on a gurney.

Cam handed him the oxygen mask. "You know the drill. Just sit here and breathe."

As soon as Jessie turned his back, Rina climbed up on the gurney next to AJ, pulled the oxygen mask down, and kissed him. She pulled away when he cut the kiss short to cough.

"Thank you for saving Petey," she said as she brushed the hair off his forehead. "Don't scare me like that again, okay?"

Jessie smiled at their kiss but frowned when AJ started coughing again. "Hey, enough of that for now," he said, checking the gauge on the oxygen tank after putting the oxygen mask back into place. "You need to go to the hospital, Bro. I don't like the sound of that wheezing." He closed his eyes and willed the memories back into the past, memories of asthma attacks and trips to the emergency room. Inhalers and breathing treatments were a part of life for AJ until they got it under control. "Hey, Cam, let's get the big hero to the hospital."

Cam had AJ lie down on the gurney, and he fastened the straps before they lifted it into the back of the ambulance.

Jessie took Petey from Rina and helped her step up into the ambulance for the ride to the hospital.

"Don't worry. I'll put the dogs in my back yard for now. We'll find something better for them tomorrow. I'll be at the hospital before you know it." After a quick kiss to her cheek, he closed the ambulance doors and watched it drive off.

He used the van to ferry all the dogs to his back yard. After returning back to Rina's, Jessie climbed into his truck as he made arrangements with the county SPCA. After completing the call, he started the engine as his lungs constricted. "God, no!" The familiar feeling of not being able to breathe had is heart pounding, the feeling he would get when his brother was having a bad asthma attack. But this time, it was even more deadly due to all the smoke AJ had inhaled. He zoomed out of the driveway, the gas pedal to the floor, not caring about anything but getting to his brother.

He answered his phone when it rang. "I'm on my way!"

Ten minutes later, he pulled up to the emergency room entrance and put his truck in neutral and pulled on the emergency brake, not bothering to shut it off or shut the door. He ran full out past the reception desk, ignoring the pain in his knee and the tightness in his chest as he heard a code blue to treatment room three. He halted when he saw the look on Rina's face, the worry and despair there for everyone to see. He grabbed her hand, and they waited. Time stood still until the doctor walked out of the treatment room with a grim look on his face. Rina dropped to the floor, sobbing as Jessie kneeled next to her and held her closely.

Picking her up off the floor, he moved to a chair and sat and settled her on his lap. He looked up at the doctor. "How bad is it?"

The doctor sat in the chair next to them. "It's not good. His asthma was aggravated by the smoke, causing his airway to be compromised. We were able to intubate him, and he is on a ventilator."

Jessie rubbed his hand up and down Rina's back as he composed himself. "Is there permanent damage to his lungs?"

"We don't know. All we can do at this point is keep him sedated and give his lungs time to heal."

Rina sobbed harder, burying her face in his shoulder.

"Shhh... It's going to be okay. He's a fighter."

Jessie looked up at the sound of running feet as Dori sped into the waiting room. "I just heard what happened. Is AJ okay?"

Rina stood and walked over to her friend and broke down into tears again. With an arm around her shoulders, Dori steered her back to the chairs.

With the girls absorbed in their conversation, Jessie looked down at his hands, surprised to discover the smears of black soot. He wiped his hands down his jeans, frowning at the black streaks. He caught Dori's gaze and motioned that he was headed to the restroom on the other side of the waiting room.

Blocked from Rina's sight, he stared into the mirror and watched the worry etch itself into his face. The saltiness of his tears surprised him. He didn't think he was capable of feeling the intense emotion needed for him to cry. In fact, he hadn't shed a tear since before he was injured in Afghanistan. Emotion had been drilled out of him; he couldn't show emotion while doing his duty as a Marine, and it had carried over into his personal life.

Leaning on the sink, he let out his emotions with a sob, a deep sound that came from the depths of his soul. How could he have stayed mad at his brother for so long? Facing the possibility that AJ could still die, he lamented the bruised ego that had kept them at odds while he served in the Marines. And over something so petty as a girl who didn't care how much she hurt the both of them with her actions.

He squinched his eyes shut and prayed, something he hadn't done since he was twelve and his parents quit forcing him and his brother to go to church every Sunday. "God, I know I don't deserve it, but I'm asking anyway. Don't let him die."

The door swung open. "Jessie? You okay in here?"

He turned away from the sight of his tear-stained face to find Dori standing in the doorway.

"Is it worse than Rina told me?"

The soles of her athletic shoes squeaked on the tile floor as she hurried over to him. She pulled him into her arms, brushing at the salty tracks on his face. For once, she didn't wince or freeze at the touch of his hands on her back.

"I'm okay. It just hit me how different it could have been. What if the ambulance showed up five minutes later? Or what if we got there five minutes later? AJ could be dead. Rina could be dead. All the dogs could be dead."

"Hey, you guys made it in time, and so did the ambulance. AJ is alive. That's the most important thing to remember." She brushed her fingers at the black marks on his face. "Why don't you clean up a bit, and I'll head to your place and pick up some clean clothes for you and Rina."

"You don't have to do that, but it is appreciated."

Chapter Six

TWO WEEKS LATER, Rina buzzed around the kitchen, pent up energy evident in her hurried movements as she waited for Jessie to finish his breakfast.

"Hurry up, would you? Don't want to be late today."

"Relax. It's only eight forty-five, and they aren't removing the intubation tube until two. I know you're anxious, but you need to sit down and relax."

"I'm just so worried. What if his lungs didn't heal? What if I have to say goodbye?"

He stopped her with his hand and motioned her to sit in the chair next to him. "Hey, no talking like that allowed. The doctors said AJ's been responding better than they expected. I'm sure everything is going to be fine."

She fiddled with the container of sugar on the table. "I know. It's just these last two weeks have gone by so slowly, and I just want to hear him tell me he loves me again. I'm scared I've found love only to lose it like I've lost everyone else."

Jessie pulled her closer and put his arms around her as she sobbed. "It's okay. AJ's not going anywhere. He's tough. It will take more than a little smoke to put him out for the count. Besides, I know he's better. I can feel it." He stood and kissed the top of her head. "Sit here and finish your coffee. I'll get these dishes cleared up. Then, go splash some water on your face or something. Can't have you showing up looking like you've been crying. He'll never forgive me."

A knock on the front door announced Dori's arrival. Shopping bags in her hands, she breezed into the kitchen and plopped into the chair Jessie had vacated moments before.

"I decided you needed something new since it's such a momentous day." She dug around in one of the bags and pulled out a turquoise blouse and a pair of black leggings. "This color will highlight the blue of your eyes. You want to look your best when AJ wakes up, right?"

"Of course, but I don't need anything new. I've got plenty of clothes in my closet. Besides, I won't have the money to pay you back until the insurance claim is settled."

Dori frowned and stuffed the clothes back into the bag. "Seriously, Rina, you need to get over this whole 'I've got to do everything myself' kick you're on. I only wanted to cheer you up. You've been so strong for AJ these last two weeks that I thought you deserved to pamper yourself a bit, and I knew you wouldn't buy anything new for yourself." Picking up the bags, she stomped toward the living room.

"Dori, wait. I'm sorry." Rina pulled on Dori's wrist to turn her around. "I really appreciate you thinking of me."

Pulling away, Dori backed up, her eyes wide with fear.

"Shit, Dor. I'm sorry. I didn't mean to startle you."

"I'm okay. I'll just put these in my car, and I'll take them back later."

"No. I'm sorry for overreacting. You were just trying to do something nice for me, and I was acting like an ungrateful brat. The stress of the last two weeks has my head reeling."

Dori dropped the bags and pulled her friend into a hug. "I understand, and you're forgiven for being a total bitch. Now, let's get you dolled up for your man. You don't want him waking up to you looking like a hag, do you?"

"I do not look like a hag," Rina replied as they hurried toward the bedroom.

Jessie watched as they retreated and smiled, glad Rina had a female friend to help her through the last couple of weeks. He knew his emotional skills could use some work. He smiled when he heard Rina yell, "Oh God. I do look like a hag!"

Jessie watched Rina as she stared at AJ, his hand in hers, as she waited for him to open his eyes. The doctors had stopped the medication that had been keeping him in the coma, wanting him to wake before they removed the intubation tube. Rina's worried gaze had him on edge. He could feel that AJ was much better, but was it enough?

He stood and stretched, trying to work out the ache in his leg. All the sitting around the last couple of weeks had him stiff and wishing for a good workout.

"AJ, baby, can you hear me?"

At Rina's question, he stared at his brother's face, willing him to open his eyes.

"There you are. Don't try to talk. They had to put in a tube to help you breathe."

When Jessie saw AJ's eyelids open slowly, he felt tears building up behind his eyes, threatening to spill over his lids. He cleared his throat to tamp them back a bit as he smiled at his brother. "I'll go let the doctor know he's awake."

A couple of strides had him out in the hall, watching as the door closed with a slight sound. Once he was sure he was out of Rina's hearing, he leaned against the wall and let the tears slide down his face. He looked up at the ceiling and tried to get his emotions under control and regulate his breathing. A hand on his arm had him straightening up and closing his hands into fists in order to defend himself.

"Jessie? Is AJ okay?"

Dori looked up at him, worry in her eyes.

"Yeah," he said before taking a deep breath with only a slight hitch. "He's awake. I need to let the doctor know."

She pulled him down the hallway. "Come on then. Let's go." When they came up to the nurse's station, she set the tray of coffee cups on the counter. "Can you page Dr. Fairfield? He needs to know AJ Monroe is awake."

Jessie was glad Dori had taken control. He didn't know if he'd be able to speak coherently around the lump in his throat. Now he knew what AJ had gone through while he waited for word if his brother would keep his leg.

Dori looked up at him. "You go compose yourself. We don't need AJ worrying about you. I'll deliver the coffee and tell him you had to hit the little boy's room."

"Thanks, Beauty," he mumbled as he strode off toward the nearest empty room, his mind whirling with 'what if' thoughts. What if AJ hadn't lived? What if he'd lost Rina? What if he'd lost the only family he had left?

The small waiting area was empty, and he could be alone and try to come to terms with his thoughts. Rubbing his hands over his face, he gave in and let his emotions bubble to the surface. First a tear, then a sob. God, he was turning into a girl with all these emotions running through him. Reminding himself AJ was awake, he prayed his brother's lungs were healed enough that he could breathe on his own.

The clang of a metal object hitting the tile floor had him sitting at attention and reaching for the gun at his hip. The hospital faded away, and he was in an Afghan city, on point for the mission: find the insurgents hiding in the village. Every doorway and shadow had the potential to hide the enemy. Searching the empty building, his attention laser-focused on the hallway stretching out in front of him. So many doors. How was he supposed to check every room without leaving himself open for attack? Where was the rest of his unit?

The whistle and boom of rockets hitting the ground outside the building didn't mask the sound of men screaming in agony. Dropping his gun, he put his hands over his ears to try and block out the sound.

"Sir? Are you okay?"

The dusty hallway gave way to the sparkling clean hospital. "What? Yeah. I'm fine."

The nurse looked at him, as if she didn't quite believe his words. "Where did you serve?"

"Shit, is it that obvious?"

"I also work at the VA hospital, so I've seen these kinds of episodes quite often. Are you talking to someone about them?"

"Jessie?"

He turned to find Dori watching him, her face troubled.

"AJ wants to see you before the doctor removes the tube."

He could feel waves of worry wash over him. Sometimes he could feel AJ's every emotion. "Okay. I'll be right there." With a sigh, he watched Dori hurry back toward his brother's hospital room. Once she was in the room and out of sight, he turned back to the nurse. "I've got it under control."

"Just remember help is there if you need it."

"Thanks. I will."

. . .

51

Jessie sat in the chair near the window, his mood brighter than it had been in months. His brother was awake and breathing on his own; he felt like he could finally relax if only for a few minutes. Dori related the dogs' daily antics to AJ, but AJ only had eyes for his fiancée, a smile on his face as he watched her laugh. Dori put her hand on AJ's arm to make a point, and Jessie almost jumped out of his chair to pull it away. Where did that come from? He'd never felt such all-consuming jealousy, not even when he caught Sasha kissing his brother. Pissed off and looking for a fight, he'd let that be the catalyst that drove him away and into the Marines. It hadn't been jealousy; it had been anger at having to hear people call him AJ, that they couldn't tell the twins apart. Feeling inadequate that he wasn't an "A" student like his brother, he let that anger fester inside until it boiled over and drove a wedge between the brothers that took him almost losing his leg to close.

He turned the chair and stared out the window over-looking the parking lot as he pushed at the anger, trying to fit it back into its box in his brain. Closing his eyes, he imagined his Beauty running her hands through his hair as she kissed him. The drone of voices was an undercurrent to the show playing out in his mind. He rubbed his hands up and down her back, and she didn't flinch, not even when his right hand reached around to grab her butt to pull her up closer to him. He was touching her, and she wasn't flinching. He never wanted it to end.

Her hand rested on his arm, seeming to burn straight into his skin. The best burn, the heat of her love pulsed from her hand to his bloodstream. His hand covered hers, pressing it deeper into his arm. Was there any better feeling?

"Jessie, wake up."

The urgent tone of her voice snapped him out of his self-induced trance. "What's wrong?" He looked up to find Rina cuddled up with AJ on the bed, fast asleep.

"I didn't want to wake you, but you'll be more comfortable at home in bed instead of sleeping in that chair." She pulled her hand out from under his arm, and he resisted the urge to shiver at the loss of heat.

Stretching his arms above his head, he yawned, trying to shake off the effects of his nap. "You're probably right. Let's head back to the house. Since Rina is sleeping here, you'll get the room to yourself tonight. We can stop and pick up something for dinner and watch a movie or something." Normally he didn't care for company, but he needed human contact. Knowing she was his everything, he wanted to spend every waking moment with her even if it was just eating takeout and watching a movie. Never before had he felt this need to keep a girl close, to protect her even if she didn't need it.

"You sure? I don't want to impose."

"You are the furthest thing from an imposition. Haven't you noticed I'm attracted to you? I know someone hurt you in the past. I would never do that."

Head down, she rummaged through her purse, looking for her keys. "Whatever," she mumbled. Pulling her keys out, she looked up to find him staring at her. "How about I stop at the drive-in for a couple of burgers and meet you at the house?"

"Sounds good. Let me get you some money…"

"Nope, my treat. You get home and relax, and I'll be there shortly with the food. Find a movie on pay-per-view or something for us to watch." She turned and stepped toward the door. "Nothing bloody, okay?"

Jessie walked in the front door and frowned at the mess that was his living room. The last two weeks, he and Rina had been spending most of their time at the hospital, sitting with his brother and not worrying about the house. He hung his keys on the hook by the door before throwing his coat on the hall tree. The couch was covered in newspapers, some still wrapped with a rubber band. "Wow. How did we let it get this bad?" He picked up the papers to drop them in the recycle bin in the kitchen, then changed his mind and took them outside to the big bin.

The room still didn't look clean, but at least you could see the furniture. Relieved to find the kitchen in better shape, he gathered plates and silverware for their food before opening the fridge to see if there was any beer. He was surprised to find it full of food, including his favorite alcoholic beverage and a bottle of wine. Dori must have done some shopping while he was with Rina sitting with his brother. Even with everything going on, she thought of something as simple as making sure there was food in the house.

Forgoing the beer for the wine, he rooted around in the junk drawer for a corkscrew, cursing when he didn't find one. What the hell did Rina do with it? Oh well. He'd figure something out after he had everything else set up. Rina enjoyed wine, so at least he had some appropriate glasses. Setting everything on the living room table, he remembered he usually used the corkscrew on his pocketknife.

Should he go ahead and open the wine? Weren't you supposed to let it breathe or something? He laughed when he stopped to check his appearance in the bathroom mirror. This wasn't a date. She hadn't given him any indication she was interested in him as anything other than a friend. He needed to get a grip.

When he heard the front door open, he rushed to the couch and plopped down, trying to look relaxed.

"Food's here," she called as she shut the door with her foot.

"Here, let me get the bags." His mouth watered at the aroma of grilled meat and onions. Setting the food on the table, he reached for the wine. "You want a glass?" he asked as he motioned with the bottle.

"Sure. That sounds nice. You pour while I divvy up the food."

After handing a filled glass to her, he punched the buttons on the remote to pull up the latest movies.

"You know what, let's watch something funny. I, for one, have had enough drama to last for a while."

As the movie played, she inched closer to him on the couch, the wine helping her overcome her fears just enough to give in to her desire for closeness until she was tucked up under his arm. Amazed at the feeling of her snuggled up into him, he relaxed and focused on the movie.

As the credits rolled across the screen, he looked down at Dori, surprised to discover her sleeping. With a smile, he brushed her hair off her face, careful not to startle her. "Hey, Beauty, wake up. You missed the end of the movie."

Her eyes opened, and she smiled.

He watched as the fear tried to creep into her face. "It's okay. No one will hurt you as long as I'm here."

She relaxed. "I know. I think it's time I told you why I came running back to Woodview."

He had a pretty good idea what she was about to say. He let her continue.

"My last relationship wasn't healthy for me. I'd finally reached the point where I was worried for my life, so I left. I threw some clothes in a suitcase and jumped in my car. Luckily, I had some money saved, and that was enough to get me here to Rina. I knew she would help me." She wiped at the tears rolling down her face. "As I drove three days to get here, I promised myself I wouldn't cry over him ever again, dammit."

"Shhh… Please don't cry." Her tears over some abusive asshat made him want to punch something. "Tell me who he is. I'll make sure he never hurts you again." He knew there was more to her story, but now wasn't the time to badger her for the rest.

"No. It's not your problem. It's mine. Now that you know, can we move forward?"

Chapter Seven

JESSIE PACED the length of the porch and back again. Dori was holed up with Rina in the bedroom, getting ready for their first official date. He'd been spending time at the shelter, helping with the dogs in order to spend time with Dori, letting her get used to him being around. There was plenty to keep him busy, as the sheriff had arrested the town drunk, Sid Nelson, for starting the fire, who in turn had implicated the former mayor in a scheme to get Rina's land. They'd released Rina's accounts, and her insurance paid out enough to rebuild the shelter better than before.

Finding the perfect first date had had him stumped until he'd driven past Woodview Mini Golf. Dinner at the drive-in and a round of mini golf would be perfect. Not too fancy and being out in the open, there was less chance of Dori being touched accidentally. He walked back and forth, worried that she'd change her mind at the last minute. A date was a big step. What was taking them so long? It was just mini golf and dinner, not a black-tie affair. He stopped and looked out over the field toward the forest as a doe and her fawn stepped out of the foliage to feed on the tender grass.

The squeal of the screen door opening brought his attention back to the front door where he found Dori standing and watching him. The girls had done something with makeup, making her chocolate brown eyes look even darker, threatening to pull him in.

"You ready?" He stopped himself before he could blurt out "finally." A quick look at his watch told him he had been waiting about ten minutes, not long at all. Holding out his hand, he waited for her to step forward while every nerve ending screamed at him to go claim her now. He knew she was the one for him, but she was nowhere close to knowing the same about him.

When her hand slid into his, the tingle traveled up his arm, making him want to stop and savor the moment when she first took his hand. "Well, then, we better get on the road. I want to get there early enough that we don't have to deal with a crowd.

After tucking her hand into the crook of his arm, they sauntered toward his truck, the paint gleaming in the afternoon sunlight. The classic vehicle was a reminder of what the Monroe boys could accomplish when they worked together.

Over the last week, he'd been working to get her used to his touch, and now she didn't even flinch when he touched her back as she hopped up into the truck. His patience was paying off, if a bit slowly. She still flinched if someone touched her unexpectedly. Every time that happened, he wanted to punch something, preferably her ex's face. He couldn't understand how anyone could raise their hand in anger toward her. From what he'd seen so far, she cared deeply for her friends and all animals. Hopefully she would come to feel the same about him. It would kill him if she couldn't find it in herself to let herself love again. Tamping down the jealousy, he concentrated on the road ahead.

Dori fiddled with her hair as she stared out the window.

"You nervous about the date?"

Dropping her hands to her lap, she turned and looked at him. "Well, yeah. It's been so long since I've gone out, much less on a date. It feels weird to be free to do whatever I want."

Gripping the steering wheel tighter, he forced his lips to curve up into a smile instead of a frown. "Well, I hope you have fun tonight. You should have told me you were nervous. I could have figured out something else for us to do." He reached over and brushed her hair behind her ear. "The thought of you being nervous or scared because of me… You know I wouldn't want that, right?" Lacing his fingers with hers, he held her hand against his thigh, the contact with her skin sending tingles through his body. Forcing himself to focus on the road, he signaled for the turn into the parking lot.

"It looks just the same. Rina and I used to spend our summers hanging out here and the drive-in. I wonder if Mr. Williams still owns it."

"I don't know. I haven't played mini golf in years." After parking, he opened the passenger door and held his hand out to his beautiful date. "Shall we?"

Grinning at him, she placed her hand into his and allowed him to lead her into the building.

An older gentleman looked up from the book he was reading at the register. "Dori Graham, is that you? You haven't changed a bit."

"Mr. Williams! I was wondering if you were still the owner." Pulling away from Jessie, she walked up to Mr. Williams and hugged him. Looking around the shop, she commented, "It looks the same except for the video games."

"Check out the one back in the corner. I think you'll be surprised."

Walking over to the area where the video games stood,

she headed for a game tucked back in the corner. "Oh my God. You still have Tempest!" she squealed as she dug around in her purse for some change.

"You and your friend Rina used to spend all afternoon pumping quarters into that old machine. You were the only two who ever played that thing."

"I can't believe you didn't get rid of it. It's got to be almost forty years old. Crap, I don't have any quarters."

Jessie held out a handful of coins. "Here, Dori. Let's start our date with some video games. I've never played this one. You can teach me."

She took the coins and fed them into the machine. "The object is to destroy the enemy. You move using the dial, and this button fires."

After a couple of quick turns, Dori found her groove and started advancing levels, leaving Jessie back in the first level. With a woo-hoo, she finished up her last turn, surprised to see her and Rina's initials still in the high-score listing. "Oh my, this brings back memories."

Jessie's heart thumped a little faster at the smile on her face. Watching her shed her inhibitions, even if only for the duration of the game, pulled him further into love with her. "Now I'll have to come and practice before I bring you here again. You're really good at this game." Kissing her temple, he willed his heartbeat back to normal. "You ready for some mini golf now?"

"Yes, and just so you know, I'll expect you to buy me a slushie halfway through the course. It's tradition."

"Anything for you, Beauty." Sauntering over to the counter, he stopped and dug out his wallet. "Two games please."

"Oh, I'm sorry. I didn't introduce you. Mr. Williams, this

is Jessie Monroe. He owns the Winter's place. Rina is marrying his twin brother."

"Is he the one who got hurt in the fire?" At her nod he commented, "I'm glad to hear he's going to be okay. You tell Rina I expect an invitation to the wedding."

"I sure will. And I'm definitely telling her about you still having Tempest."

After choosing their balls and putters, they stepped out of the building into the afternoon sun. A few couples were at different holes along the course. There would be more as the night grew closer; there weren't many date options in a small town.

"It's a perfect day to be outside. You want to go first, or should I?" Dori asked as they approached the first hole.

"Ladies first."

"Okay. Just to let you know, I might be good at Tempest, but I suck at mini golf."

"I used to be pretty good at this. I'll give you some pointers."

"Smug much?" she asked with a laugh.

"No. Just confident."

Lining up her bright orange ball, she gave it a tap with the club, frowning when it bounced back toward her.

"See. I never could get my swing right."

Picking up her ball, he placed it back on the tee. "Here, let me help you with that." Placing her in front of him, he reached around her, putting his hands over hers. "Is this okay?" he whispered into her ear. He smiled at her shiver.

"Yes."

"Okay, relax and let me control your putt so you can feel how I do it."

She giggled. "Oh, yeah, I can feel it. It's poking me in the butt!"

"Sorry about that. That's what happens when I get close to you. Ignore it and concentrate on your swing."

"Yeah, sure."

They continued along the course. After playing the ninth hole, Dori tallied up their scores. "Wow, you hit par on every hole but one. You are good at this."

"The only reason I missed that one is because someone kept distracting me." He looked over at the snack bar. "Isn't it time for your slushie? What flavor do you want?"

"Dr. Pepper if they still have it. If not, surprise me."

"I'll be right back."

Once he reached the counter, he watched Dori sit on a bench and bounce her golf ball. When he returned with her drink, she was staring off across the course. Without thinking, he put his hand on her shoulder. He frowned when she jumped away from his touch. "Shit. Sorry, Dori. I didn't mean to startle you."

"God, when will I be able to not jump out of my skin when someone startles me?"

"You know I'd never do anything to hurt you, right?"

"Yeah. I just wish I could get over being so jumpy. Did they have my Dr. Pepper?"

He handed her the cup in his hand. "We can leave if you want."

"No. I want to finish the game. I am having a great time with you."

Teeing up her ball, she swung too hard, and the ball returned to her after bouncing off the back of the hole. "Geez, why can't I play this stupid game?" Kicking the ball, it traveled to the hole and dropped in. "Did you see that?"

Jessie laughed. "Now you know how to get a hole-in-one. Just give it a kick."

They finished their game and then stopped at the drive-in

for burgers. Other than when Dori flinched away from his touch, he was pleased with their first date. The quick kiss in the kitchen before they went to their respective rooms did nothing to put out the fire in his blood. He hoped they would eventually get to a place where he could love her physically.

As the weeks passed, they continued with the dates. Each goodnight kiss better and longer then the last. The first time she kissed him in front of Rina and his brother, he wanted to do a victory dance. They'd made so much progress that he was seriously considering telling her he loved her and wanted to marry her.

The only damper on his mood was the frequency of his nightmares. They'd increased to two or three a week. He really needed one of his camping trips to get his head back on straight. But that would have to wait. AJ and Rina were getting married, and he was helping his brother get the renovations to Rina's house done so they could move in after the wedding. Surely he could keep it together for another couple of weeks.

Chapter Eight

JESSIE STOOD at the front of the church next to AJ, smiling as his brother shifted his weight from foot to foot. "Relax, Bobo. They're still seating guests."

"What if she…?"

"What if she what? Doesn't show? Runs screaming from the church?" He chuckled. It was funny that the normally serious AJ was letting his nerves get the better of him. "Relax before you give yourself an asthma attack. That would ruin the day for sure."

"I just want to get this done. What is taking so long?"

"It's been five minutes. Just relax."

His attention shifted as the double doors at the back of the church opened and the organ music changed, quieting the guests. Dori stood framed by the doorway, a nervous smile on her face. The rest of the world dropped away when her gaze met his, and her nervousness vanished.

He couldn't believe it had only been two months since the night she had opened up to him about the abuse. She hadn't told him everything, just enough so he understood how hard it had been for her to trust him. He grinned when she took her

64

place on the other side of the alter and blew him a kiss. His attention turned back to the doors when the music changed again. Time to get his brother married.

Dori watched Rina dancing with her new husband, wondering if she would ever feel safe enough to let Jessie know how she felt about him. She had been honored to help her friend celebrate her marriage, but standing up at the front of the church had been nerve-wracking. After so many years of trying to not be noticed, it was hard to be up there on display.

Turning from the dance floor, she stumbled from a combination of alcohol and her heels. Jessie caught her and kept her from falling to the floor.

"I need to go get my flip flops before I break an ankle. I left them up in Rina's room in the house." She kissed him and stumbled toward the house, humming and thinking about Jessie's arms wrapped around her when they danced to the slow songs. She hurried up the stairs after slipping out of her shoes. She grabbed her flip flops out of the bag and put them on before stopping to check her reflection in the mirror. Her eyes sparkled, and her face was flushed from dancing; she looked happy. She ran down the stairs, yearning for the feel of Jessie's arms around her again.

She froze when a voice from her past whispered in her ear. "I finally have you alone. Your soldier boy can't save you now."

Before she could scream, a hand covered her mouth, mashing her lips against her teeth. Her assailant wrapped his other arm around her and pinned her to his side.

"You left. I didn't give you permission to leave. You'll pay for that," he growled as he dragged her down the porch steps, toward his van.

. . .

Jessie stood at the bar, waiting for Dori to return from changing her shoes. With a glance at his watch, he finished the beer in his hand, handing the empty bottle to the bartender, Jay.

"You want another?" Jay asked as he tossed the bottle into the recycle bin.

"No. I'm going to go see what's taking Dori so long. I'm headed into the house if anybody is looking for me," he answered before walking off. It was quiet closer to the house, away from the party. His hand on the screen door handle, he stopped when he heard a distant scream. That sounded like Dori. Running around to the back, he hoped the scream was just someone having some fun, but the sinking feeling in his gut had him convinced it was something much more serious.

Rounding the corner, he spied someone dragging Dori toward the barn where a van sat idling. She managed to wriggle one arm loose and hit her abductor on the side of the head with her arm, making him loosen his grip enough that she got about one half step away as she screamed. The guy grabbed her and shoved her into the waiting van, pulling the door closed as the van took off for the road.

Cam hurried up to Jessie. "Was that a scream? What's happened?"

"Give me my keys. Someone just took Dori!" Jessie yelled, catching the keys when Cam tossed them to him. He jumped into his truck and took off, spewing gravel behind him as he tried to keep the van in sight. When he reached the road, the van was gone.

Not giving up, Jessie drove through town, looking everywhere. Intent on his search, he didn't notice the siren and flashing lights of the state police car behind him. The police car pulled around him and blocked the street, forcing him to stop. Jesse banged his hands on the steering wheel as he muttered about stupid cops keeping him from finding Dori. He wasn't thinking clearly as he jumped out of the car and stalked toward the police car, his hands clenched into fists.

The officer got out of the car and ducked when Jessie took a swing at her. "Dammit, Jessie! I'm here to help. Calm down," she said forcefully. "If you don't calm down, I will cuff you and stick you in the back of my car until you cool off."

Jessie clenched his fists but kept them at his side, knowing that Brynn would follow up on her threat. "They took her, Brynn. They shoved her in a van and took her," he said, trying to keep the sob that wanted to break free out of his voice, not quite succeeding. "It was a dark green delivery van, fairly new with no decals or logos visible on it."

"We'll find her, Jessie," Brynn said as she scribbled furiously in her notebook before she turned back to her car and put out an APB on the van. "Did you see the guy who grabbed her?" she asked, trying to get as much information as possible.

"No. By the time I got to the front of the house, he was shoving her into the van. He had longish blond hair and was wearing a dark suit." Jessie rubbed his hands down his face. "That's all I could see."

Brynn relayed the information then opened the back door of her cruiser. "Sit down and tell me everything that happened."

"She told me she was headed to the house to grab her flip flops. We both brought a change of clothes with us today so we could change to take care of the shelter tonight. I finished my beer and decided to surprise her in the house." Jessie ran his hands through his hair, making it stand straight up. "Jesus,

Brynn, I heard her scream." He had to stop for a moment to calm himself; remembering her scream made him feel like he was going to be sick. "I ran around to the front of the house and saw her being shoved into the van." He stood and walked to the back bumper of the cruiser and stared off at the horizon. "You have to find her, Brynn."

Brynn put her hand on Jessie's shoulder. "Is there anyone who you think might be behind this?"

"She is afraid of her ex-boyfriend. A couple of months ago, she confessed to me that he was physically abusive. She wouldn't tell me his name, but I think Rina knows him. Things had been going so well between us I didn't want to push it. Now I wish I had."

His cell phone pinged, notifying him of a text. "Did u find her?"

"No," he typed back. "Brynn put out an APB. Headed back."

Cam texted back, "Will wait 4 u to tell A & R."

Jessie turned and looked back at Brynn. "I have to get back and tell AJ and Rina what's happened."

Jessie pulled into Rina's driveway, dreading ruining AJ and Rina's wedding day, with Brynn pulling in behind him. He stared at Rina's house, trying to get the image of Dori being shoved into the van out of his mind.

Cam walked up and asked, "Jessie? You okay?"

Jessie looked at him, his face dark with rage. He held on to the anger, feeding it to keep himself from bawling like a baby. "Can you go get AJ and Rina? I don't want to announce this in front of all the guests."

"Sure," Cam replied before he turned and walked back toward the party.

Ten minutes later, AJ and Rina walked up, all smiles and holding hands. When he saw the look on Jessie's face, AJ asked, "What's wrong?" He looked back and forth between Jessie and Brynn. "Who's hurt?"

Jessie took a deep breath to steady his nerves. "Dori is gone."

"What do you mean Dori's gone?" Rina asked as she started to panic. "Where is she?"

Jessie looked her in the eye and told her the truth. "Somebody took her against her will." He grabbed her hands, needing her to understand.

She pulled her hands out of his and then turned and ran back to the party, the others following at her heels. She went up to an older man in a suit. "Where is that piece of shit you call a son? He followed her back here, didn't he?" She turned and looked back at AJ as if to gain strength from his nearness before turning back toward the man. "Do you know how he treated her?" she screamed at him. "Do you know he beat her with a belt?" His face visibly whitened at Rina's question.

Jessie's face turned red, and he had to work to keep his hands from going around the guy's neck, the thought of Dori being beaten with a belt making him sick. He knew it was bad, but a belt? The anger crept back in, and he took a step toward him, wanting to plow his fist into his face. Maybe that would keep him from feeling so helpless.

AJ and Cam stepped in front of him. "Take it easy, Jess," AJ said. "Let's hear what he has to say before you beat him to a pulp."

"Mr. Belham, you better find Ty and get him to bring her back. I couldn't believe it when I saw you here today. I know you were a friend of my grandfather's, but with what Ty has done, you better leave."

"I'm sorry, Rina. I had no idea it was that bad. I knew they had problems." His shoulders sagged as he turned and slowly walked toward the driveway. Stopping in front of

Jessie, he looked up at his face. "I'm sorry. If I hear from Ty, I will let you all know."

Jessie put up his hand to signal that he wouldn't go after him. He started pacing, anger and fear coursing through him. "He better not hurt her," he ground out between clenched teeth. "Or I will come for you." He stalked off, walking back toward the house to change into his fatigues and a t-shirt so he could start searching for her, his heart a lump of ice in his chest.

Dori punched and kicked, trying to get away from Ty even after he shoved her into the van. "You hurt me and Jessie will find you, you asshole," she said as she glared at him. "He won't let you hurt me."

She braced herself as the van lurched forward, the cargo area empty except for a large toolbox behind the driver's seat. Recognizing the driver, she screamed at him, "Tony, you son of a bitch. You realize this is kidnapping, don't you? You're just as guilty as Ty, and you both will be going to jail. That's if you're still alive after Jessie gets done with you."

Ty grew tired of listening to Dori gush about this Jessie guy, so he grabbed her throat and squeezed until she passed out. "Don't you ever shut up?" he muttered as he tied her hands together in front of her before grabbing another rope to tie her ankles.

Dori opened her eyes just enough to see what Ty was doing. When he moved to grab her feet, she kicked up, catching his chin with her foot. It knocked him on his ass, and she lunged for the door, pulling it open and jumping out onto the road. Dori hit the pavement hard and held her bound wrists to her chest as she rolled to a stop. Attempting to get to her feet, she staggered a few steps before losing her balance and falling to the ground. She tried to get up, but Ty was on top of her before she could get her feet under her, the van screeching to a halt down the road.

Ty grabbed her arm and hauled her up. "Bitch, you're going to pay for that," he growled as he raised his arm and slapped her face before he pulled her toward the van.

Dori glared at him, vowing that she would get away from him and back to Jessie. She couldn't remember one reason why she thought she was in love with him when they left town.

Ty shoved her into the van, not caring when he slammed her face into the tool box, splitting open her cheek. "Soldier boy won't love you so much when I get done with you," he goaded her. "You think he's going to love a beat-up hag like you?"

As she listened to Ty's ranting, she decided she wasn't going to take his abuse anymore. Holding her hands over the cut in her cheek she ridiculed him, "Big man has to hit a woman who's tied up? You can't even fight fair with me. What's the matter? You afraid a girl can get the better of you?"

He grabbed her arm, squeezing until her hand started going numb, then threw her back against the side of the van, her shoulder hitting the inner fender well with a sickening pop.

Dori stayed where she landed, the pain bringing tears to her eyes. "You can't break me," she sobbed. "I'm not that scared young girl you controlled for years. I've grown up, and I won't cower in front of you ever again!" The van lurched when it hit a pothole, driving Dori's shoulder into the floor and causing a bright hot flare of agony. She closed her eyes and tried to ride out the pain, laying her head on the floor of the van and waiting for whatever Ty was going to do next as she prayed that Jessie would find her soon.

Jessie strode out to his truck, his service revolver on his hip and his hunting rifle hanging across his back. He stopped when he saw Brynn waiting by his truck. "Don't try to stop me, Brynn. I'm doing this with or without your approval. I have to find her," he said as he climbed into his truck. "I was going to ask her to marry me tonight."

"You call me when you find him." She didn't bother reminding him to wait for her to get there. She knew he would get Dori away from Ty no matter the cost. "Please, try to keep yourself under control. The main thing is to get Dori back safe and sound. Let the system punish him."

AJ ran up, now dressed in jeans, a t-shirt, and his running shoes. "Let's go, Bro," he said with his hand on the passenger door handle.

"Nope. You are not coming with me, AJ. You just got married. I'm not taking you away from Rina on your wedding day."

"Don't give me that, Jess. I can help you find her."

"I'm trained for this, AJ. You're not. Besides, it wasn't that long ago you were in the hospital."

Chapter Nine

JESSIE WATCHED the sun peek over the horizon as he sipped his coffee. He looked out over the fields, allowing himself to imagine Dori walking toward him from the trail to Rina's house.

He'd searched for Dori non-stop for two days, only stopping when he almost fell asleep waiting at a traffic light. He'd ignored his brother's questions when he walked into the house, going directly to his bedroom and collapsing on the bed. Two hours later and he was wide awake, the nightmares making it impossible for him to sleep. They were the same bloody dreams, but now they included Dori's screams as she was shoved into a van.

The squeak of the screen door brought him back to the present. He looked up to find Rina walking toward him with the coffeepot in her hand.

"Want some more coffee?" she asked with a yawn. "Did you sleep at all?" She filled his cup and set the pot on the table.

"I'm not in the mood to be social right now, Rina." He

didn't want to hurt her feelings, but he just wanted to be left alone.

Ignoring him, she continued to talk. "How about some breakfast? Have you eaten anything the last couple of days?"

"No, and I'm not hungry. I'm fine. Now go away."

"Jessie, quit shoving me away. I'm not going anywhere." She pulled her chair closer to him, taking his hand in hers. "You'll find her. You have to believe that."

"It feels like someone has sliced me in half. Don't take this the wrong way, but this feels worse than when AJ was in the hospital. At least I could feel that he was still with me…in here." He tapped his chest. "This is worse. I can't feel her like that, and it scares me. What if she is gone forever?"

"Don't think like that. You will find her. I'm sure of it." She hugged him.

"I was going to ask her to marry me after the reception. Do you think she would have said yes?"

"Of course she'd say yes. She loves you. Now, how about some breakfast? You need fuel if you're going to go out searching. Why don't you shower, and I'll have bacon and eggs ready when you're finished."

The hot water pummeled his back, easing the tense muscles as he mentally reviewed the list of possible hiding places he'd already checked. He was running out of ideas, and he was afraid he was running out of time. Even with the state-wide APB out on the van, there had been no new leads. It was as if the van had vanished into thin air, leading him to believe they were somewhere close. But where?

He leaned his head back against the tile, closing his eyes to mentally trace his planned search for the day, a route that covered most of the state park south of town. The patter of water against the cool tile relaxed him in a way he thought impossible.

Parking his truck off the side of the dirt road behind some trees and rocks, he pulled his gear out of the back and checked his gun and ammunition. Satisfied he was as prepared as he could be, he crept along the seldom-used trail leading to the abandoned hunting cabin. He'd stumbled across the cabin on one of his first treks through the park, looking for a good place for a campsite. The structure was a ramshackle one-room cabin built around 1900 that contained a small stove and a cot with an outhouse behind it.

A bit of bright pink in the tall grass to the right of the trail caught his attention. Picking up the flip flop, he knew he was in the right place. The forest was eerily quiet, the silence broken by the snapping of a twig as he stepped down the path. A couple of miles from the road, the only way to reach the cabin was on foot. Sitting on a small hill, its elevated position gave a clear line of sight to the tree line, making it a perfect hideout. The rocky terrain of the west side of the park kept the casual hikers and campers away.

Jessie picked a vantage point just inside the forest behind a fallen tree, hiding him from anyone looking out from the cabin. A shadow moved back and forth in front of the window, the wavy glass making a positive identification impossible.

Every nerve ending in his body screamed for him to move, to charge the cabin, but he knew that posed too much of a risk to Dori if she was in there. When the door opened, he ducked down, hiding himself as much as possible. He watched as one of the men he'd seen with the van walked over to a boulder and relieved himself, his back to Jessie.

Through the open door, a scream from the building had him straining to stay hidden as the man yelled, "Shut up, bitch. No one can hear you out here except for the animals, and that screech probably scared them all away."

"Fuck you, Tony. You better hope Jessie doesn't find you. He's a marine, and he'll hurt you. Bad."

"He'll never find us out here. Besides, as soon as Ty gets back, we're leaving."

Using all his training, Jessie moved in closer, making as little noise as possible. His rifle in his hand, he crept closer, finally swinging his rifle like a bat and bringing the gun stock into contact with the creep's head with a sickening crunch.

"Dori," he yelled as he ran to the cabin, "I'm here for you, Beauty."

He stood inside the door, letting his eyes adjust to the dim interior, the only light from the lone window and the open door. At his yell, Dori sat up, and the blanket covering her slid down to reveal her arm hanging loosely from her shoulder. Someone had made a temporary sling out of a strip ripped from the bottom of her dress to hold her arm still. Her face was covered in blood, crusty and dried.

"Oh God. What did they do to you?"

"Never mind. We have to go. If we're still here when Ty gets back, we're both dead."

Sitting next to her on the cot, he brushed the hair out of her face, frowning at the bruising and blood. Holding her face in his hands, he kissed her. Oblivious to everything except his love sitting in front of him, he didn't hear the footsteps approaching.

"I told you what would happen if I found you with him again."

Jessie felt the bullet whiz past his face and watched in horror as it struck Dori in the eye. She sagged in his arms as blood poured down her face.

"No!" he screamed as he gathered her in his arms. "It's going to be okay, Beauty." Staring at the man who'd shot his Dori, he stood and took a step toward the door. "You better kill me now. If you don't, I will hunt you down like the animal you are, and I will end you."

"Glad to oblige," Ty commented as he pulled the trigger again.

He dropped to his knees, carefully laying Dori's lifeless body on the floor as the pain spread through his chest. "Love you, Beauty."

"Jessie, unlock this door! What the hell is going on in there?" Rina yelled as she pounded on the bathroom door.

Cold water pounded his head and shoulders as the door crashed open, his brother and Rina looking in at him.

It was a dream, a nightmare. He couldn't believe he'd fallen asleep standing up in the shower.

AJ twisted the handles to turn off the water. "Jess, what happened?"

"I must have fallen asleep and had a nightmare."

"It must have been a doozy. You were screaming Dori's name."

The memory of Dori's face, eye gone and covered in blood made him shiver, and he wanted to be sick. He had to find her soon.

He grabbed the towel Rina held out to him. "Thanks. I'm okay now." When neither one of them moved to exit the room, he continued, "Could I get some privacy? I swear I won't fall asleep again."

Rina reached up and cupped his face. "You know you can talk to me about anything, right? And your brother too. We're both here for you."

"I'm okay. Now give a guy some privacy, will ya?"

Jessie stared into his coffee as he pushed the eggs and bacon around on his plate.

"Jess, you need to eat. You're going to need fuel if you're going to rescue Dori." She poured more coffee into his mug.

"Fine." He shoveled eggs in his mouth, chewing and swallowing quickly, afraid if he thought about it he'd end up emptying his stomach. She was right. He wouldn't be any good to his Beauty if he didn't eat.

Shoving the last strip of bacon into his mouth, he chewed and swallowed, washing it down with a swig of coffee. "Satisfied?" he asked as he looked at Rina.

"Yes. Now get going and find our girl." She hugged him from behind whispering in his ear, "I have a feeling you're going to find her today."

Breaking out of her hug, he stood and looked at his brother. "AJ, I'm going to check out the state park today. You know cell service is spotty out there, so don't panic if I don't call in every hour."

"Call Brynn and make sure she knows where you're searching. You're not invincible."

"Yes, mother."

"I'm serious. Now, get out there and find your girl."

Trees and hills rushed past in a blur as he drove down the old logging road. Eerily reminiscent of his earlier nightmare, he couldn't shake the feeling that he was close. Maybe she really was in the old hunting cabin.

An area of flattened vegetation on the side of the road caught his attention as he slowed for a curve. Pulling off the road, he picked a spot where his vehicle wouldn't be easily spotted. He jogged back to the spot that had caught his attention and followed what could be tracks left by a car. The tracks led to a small meadow where it looked like a vehicle had been parked.

Scanning the woods for any clue as to what someone would be doing parked out in the middle of nowhere, a splash of pink among the green of the grass caught his attention.

No way. It couldn't be. Could it?

With a shiver, he picked up the flip flop. The placement and everything was just like in his dream. Spurred by his find, he hurried down the trail toward the cabin. Watching the cabin, he was surprised to see the scene play out exactly like his dream, down to the guy coming out to pee on the boulder. Using his rifle as a club, he knocked him out and ran toward the door.

Standing in the doorway to let his eyes adjust to the dim interior, he heard Dori call out to him. "Jessie! Oh my God! I knew you'd find me!" Despite worrying that events would continue following his dream, he still couldn't keep himself from stopping and kissing Dori.

"Come on, Beauty. We have to go now," he urged as he stood, placing Dori on her feet.

His stomach twisted when he heard Ty's words. "I told you what would happen if I found you with him again."

He stepped in front of Dori as he heard the shot ring out, but this time it sounded different, as if it was from farther away. Time slowed to a crawl as he waited for the burning pain of a bullet burrowing into his flesh. Afraid the bullet would kill him, he murmured, "Love you forever, Beauty," finally admitting his true feelings.

"Love you too, Jess."

Instead of the whiz of a bullet, he heard a thump as something hit the floor.

"Jessie, you okay?"

He turned to find Brynn standing over Ty lying on the floor, blood pooling around his prone body.

"Yeah, but Dori's hurt."

"Don't worry. The medivac chopper is on its way."

Relief coursing through his veins, the sound of his heart thumping along in his chest drowned out all other sounds as his knees threatened to collapse under him. Dori was safe. He didn't have to watch her life pour out of a wound in her head. He barely turned enough to sit on the bed when his knees actually gave out.

Even knowing she was safe, all he could think about was seeing her slack in his arms, the light gone out of her eyes. Tears streaked his face as he tried to force that picture from his mind.

Chapter Ten

THE SQUEAK of a rubber sole on the tile floor outside the room was the only indication Jessie wasn't the only one awake at one a.m. Dori dozed in a drug-induced slumber to combat the pain of her injuries. A broken cheekbone and a dislocated shoulder were the worst of it, with a myriad of other bruises and abrasions covering most of her body.

He tried to sleep, but the image of her lifeless body from his nightmare wouldn't let him rest. Thank God AJ had told Brynn where he was going to be searching that day or his nightmare would have come true. As usual, he let his penchant for charging in without considering the consequences put someone he loved in harm's way. He didn't deserve to have someone like his Beauty in his life.

With the lightest of touches, Jessie brushed the hair off her forehead. "I'm so sorry I failed you, Beauty. You deserve a man who can protect you, and I'm obviously not him."

With one last look at her resting peacefully, he squared his shoulders and walked out of the room, determined to stay out of her life. She deserved better than what a broken-down Marine could give her.

.　.　.

Dori woke to the nurse checking her IV. Nurse? IV? The events of the previous day filled her mind, bringing a smile to her face. She had known Jessie would find her. With a vague memory of him sleeping in the recliner next to her bed, she turned her head to find the chair empty, a blanket folded neatly on the seat.

"Where's Jessie?"

"He left a couple of hours ago. I'm sure he just went home to get some sleep."

"Oh, okay." Disappointed at his absence, she decided it was time to assess the damage Ty had wrought. "Can you help me to the restroom?"

"Sure, honey. Let me get you some soap and a toothbrush."

Running her fingertips over her face, she grimaced at the dried blood and the pain in her cheek.

The nurse bustled back into the room, a small caddy in her hands. "Here's the soap and stuff I mentioned. Would you like some help getting cleaned up?"

"That would be wonderful. Oh, and what is your name? I don't want to just call you nurse."

"I'm Martha. I'll be going off shift in about thirty minutes, so let's get you cleaned up."

After helping her to the sink, Martha turned on the water and readied the soap. "Now, it's not as bad as it looks."

Her stomach churned at the sight of her face. Bruised and battered, the white of the bandage over her right cheek high-lighted the purple around her right eye.

"God, no wonder he left. I look hideous."

"No talking like that. I'm sure he'll be back any minute. He didn't even want to let you out of his sight for the x-

82

rays." She lathered up the soap into the washcloth and handed it to Dori. "You have twelve stitches in your cheek and a broken cheekbone, but you don't need to worry. We have the best plastic surgeon in the state on staff, and he stitched you up himself. I'm sure there won't be much of a scar at all."

That's how she'd known Ty was going to kill her. He'd never hit her where someone could see the results. He'd always chosen places that would be hidden by her clothing.

Once the blood was gone and Martha had helped her brush out her hair, she at least felt somewhat human. After introducing her to the day nurse, Martha checked her IV one last time and slipped out of the room.

Where was he? Why wasn't he back yet?

She looked up when the door opened, slightly disappointed to see Rina and AJ.

"Oh my God. Look what he did to your poor face," her friend exclaimed as she hurried toward the hospital bed. "Where's Jessie? I thought he'd be here."

"I don't know. The nurse said he left in the middle of the night, and he hasn't been back."

AJ dropped the bag containing clothes for Dori and pulled out his phone. He dialed his brother's cell as he walked out of the room.

Rina pulled the chair closer to the bed. "I'm sure Jessie will be back any minute. He probably fell asleep and forgot to set an alarm. I don't think he slept much while you were gone."

"I just have this weird feeling he's not coming back."

They could hear AJ leaving a voicemail for Jessie. "Where are you? Call me when you get this."

He strode into the room, muttering about how his brother was an idiot. "Something's up with him. I think we need to

83

have a brotherly chat." He kissed Rina. "Do you want to go with me or stay here?"

"I'll stay. I don't want Dori to be alone." After kissing him on the cheek, she rummaged through the bag. "You'll feel better once you're in your own clothes. Let's get you changed."

The quiet of the forest didn't soothe him the way it normally did. As Jessie stared out across the river, the image of Dori beaten and bloody haunted his thoughts. He was trained in combat, but he couldn't keep his friends and family safe. First there was Rina's problems with the former mayor who wanted her land. He had been off on one of his camping trips when Rina almost died from an infection, and then there was the fire that almost killed his brother. He should have been able to keep both of those from happening, but he had been too wrapped up in his own head to be aware of the danger. Then he'd almost gotten Dori killed by thinking he could play the hero all by himself. He leaned back against a tree and rubbed his hands over his face. Maybe it was time to admit he didn't deserve Dori's love.

The echo of a gunshot had him dropping to the ground and crawling toward some underbrush that could be used as cover. How did they find him here? Where was his gear? His gun? Why did he leave the base without even his radio?

Concentrating on the gunfire coming from the west, he didn't hear the enemy soldier creeping up behind him. When the hand landed on his shoulder, he reacted, his training over-riding conscious thought. Grabbing the guy's wrist, he pulled him down and flipped him, landing on top of the other soldier. Frantically searching the ground for the enemy's gun, he placed his hand over the offender's neck, squeezing slightly to keep him pinned down.

"Jessie! Dammit, Jess. It's me. What the hell are you doing?"

Why was this guy speaking English with an American accent? He must have received some intense training to sound like he was from the Midwest.

"Jessie, it's me, AJ."

The fog in his brain lifted, letting him see reality instead of the hell he endured over in Afghanistan. What the hell was AJ doing in the war zone? Shaking his head, his mind cleared, and he realized he was in Indiana, not overseas.

"AJ? What the hell?"

Lifting his hand from his brother's neck, he crab-walked backward away from him. "Oh shit. I'm sorry, Bobo. You shouldn't sneak up on me like that." Standing, he turned his back to his brother, not wanting him to see the anguish he felt.

AJ coughed to clear his throat. "I've been yelling for ten minutes. How did you not hear me?"

"I was trying to tune out the world. That's kinda the point."

"Dori's been asking for you. You've been gone for hours. Luckily Brynn saw you driving out this way this morning or I'd still be looking for your sorry ass."

"You obviously haven't learned I can't be trusted. I'm not the reliable Jessie you grew up with."

"What bullshit is that? You've always been one of the most reliable guys I know."

Clenching his fists, he paced and worked to block the images of Dori from his mind. "I've got issues you don't know about, and being around Dori isn't helping."

"It's the PTSD, isn't it? Is it getting worse?"

"How do you know about that?"

"Besides the fact that I'm your twin and I just know things, I talked to your doctor when you were in the hospital in Germany."

"Dammit. He told me he couldn't talk to you about it."

"He thought he was talking to you."

"How did you convince him you were me?"

Squaring his shoulders, AJ slipped into what he thought of as his Jessie side. "Seriously, I can 'do you' better than you can. I'm a marine, and I know best." Dropping the act, he continued. "I only did it because I knew there was more going on, but you wouldn't talk about it."

Dropping to sit down on a log, Jessie ran his fingers through his hair. "Up until a few months ago, my camping trips were enough to keep it under control, but then I met Dori, and I started to lose control over it. As you just saw, it has gotten worse since Dori was kidnapped. I feel like I'm unraveling, and I can't stop it."

"Have you talked to anyone about it?"

"No, and I don't plan to. All they want to do is push some pills at me and shove me out the door. I tried that in the beginning, and it didn't help."

Sitting beside his brother, AJ turned to face him. "How about trying a different doctor, not through the VA. I can call a friend of mine and get a referral."

"You have a friend who's a shrink?"

"I met him through my doctor when I needed some information for my book."

"You see a shrink? Why?"

"Guilt mostly. Guilt for driving you to join the Marines."

"Me becoming a Marine had nothing to do with you or that bimbo. I needed something that was separate from you.

After so many years of being one of the Monroe Twins, I needed to find something that was just me."

AJ stared at his brother. "Why didn't you tell me? Wait, let's get back on topic—your current issues. I need you to promise me you'll talk to someone. What if I can't get through to you next time? And if you don't deal with it, there will be a next time."

Jessie stood and resumed his pacing. "You're right. I can't deal with it on my own anymore. Get me a name, and I'll make an appointment."

"I'll make your appointment. You just worry about keeping it together until you can talk to someone."

"What, you don't trust me?" Jessie asked with a grin.

"Nope. Not about this."

Chapter Eleven

JESSIE WALKED through the back door behind his brother, flinching at the hurt in Rina's eyes. "I'm sorry I took off like that."

"Why are you apologizing to me? Save it for Dori. She's been asking about you since this morning."

Pulling his friend into a hug, he whispered in her ear, "I'm an ass, and I'll make it up to both of you."

"Make what up to me? You saved my best friend from her psychotic ex. That had nothing to do with me."

"We'll talk later. I need to go make things right with Dori."

"We've got her set up on the couch. We'll work on dinner and give you two some time to talk."

With a squeeze, he let her go and took a deep breath to prepare himself to see the hurt in Dori's eyes.

He stopped at the entrance to the living room and stared at Dori propped up on the sofa, the remote for the television in her hand.

"Hey, Beauty."

The relief in her eyes squeezed his heart like a lemon,

forcing out every drop of blood. "Jessie," she said with a sigh. "I was so worried about you. You took off without a word to anyone."

"I'm so sorry I made you worry. There were some things I needed to think about, so I took off for the state park to clear my head."

"Come over here and sit down. I'll get a crick in my neck looking up at you over there." She sat up and swung her legs off the couch, patting the cushion next to her.

"I…" He cleared his throat and tried again. "I'm sorry I wasn't able to find you sooner."

"It wasn't your fault I couldn't see what Ty was really like until it was too late. At least you know why I flinched whenever someone touched me."

"Someday you'll find someone worthy of your attention, not some loser like your ex. Someone who will treat you like you deserve." He ignored her look of confusion and continued. "You deserve to find a man who will love and cherish you, someone who can protect you."

Dori stared at him in shock. "Why, what's wrong with the man who's sitting right here in front of me?"

"I'm no good for anyone, especially you." He stood and faced away from her, shoving his hands in his pockets. "I'll see you later."

Dori stared at the television, the colorful images reflecting in her eyes as she pondered Jessie's statement. Something kept Jessie from letting her get too close, as if he were afraid of intimacy. She knew that wasn't the issue. They'd shared some intense kisses and had almost taken things further than some serious petting, but after she'd been kidnapped by Ty, it was as if Jessie didn't want to get close to her. The yearning in his eyes was in direct opposition to his actions. Was he turned off by her injuries? Would he return to the previous version of Jessie who was attentive and loving after her face returned to normal?

Grumpy and frustrated with his actions, she pulled her yoga mat out of her bag and prepared to do some basic poses, hoping that would bring some peace of mind. Wincing at the pull on the wrenched muscles in her shoulder, she switched poses.

Dori lost her concentration when the front door slammed.

"What are you doing?" Rina demanded, her hands on her hips.

"Preparing to run a marathon. What does it look like I'm doing? It's just some simple yoga to relieve some stiffness."

"You are supposed to be resting and healing, not over-exerting yourself. The doctor told you nothing strenuous for a week, especially with your shoulder."

Dori stood and turned to face her friend. "I know that, but I'm going crazy lying around all day." Dropping down into another pose, Dori hid her face from her friend.

"Did Jessie come and talk to you? If he ducked out without explaining himself…"

"He was here earlier. Though I don't buy his explanation. He said I deserve a man who would love me. I know we hadn't known each other that long, but I thought we were heading toward deepening our relationship, and I know he was thinking the same. No matter what he says now, I saw the ring box sitting out on his dresser about a week before you and AJ got married. Am I that hideous now that he can't love me?"

Rina stood, her arms folded across her chest. "Something is going on, and I'm going to find out what if I have to sick

AJ on him. Seriously, sometimes these Monroe men are a pain in my butt."

"Rina, don't. Don't guilt him into anything. I'm sure he'll tell me why the sudden change when he's ready. I'm just so frustrated right now."

"Okay, if you're sure."

"Yeah. Besides, I'm going to be too busy to worry about it starting tomorrow." Dori sat and patted the yoga mat next to her. "Sit down. I've got an idea I need to discuss with you."

Chapter Twelve

JESSIE PARKED his truck in front of the shelter, turning off the engine but not exiting the vehicle. Four weeks of therapy appointments and they had made progress, but it was slower than he wanted. The appointments always left him feeling a bit off-kilter until his brain had a chance to process everything they discussed. When the therapist had suggested he take a leave of absence from his job, he almost walked out of the appointment right then and there. He hated to admit it, but the reduction in his stress levels had helped, and the meds took the edge off, but he still had episodes. Fortunately, none were as bad as the one when he came back to himself with his hands around his brother's neck. They were making the most progress with his ability to feel an episode coming on, and he could do some exercises that stopped it or kept it from becoming a full-blown, not knowing what he was doing, episode.

Today, his therapist had again recommended he get a therapy dog. He wasn't sure about how effective that would be. Spending time at Rina's shelter seemed to help, but having a dog full-time? He was making progress in his treatment, but most days he didn't feel capable of taking care of himself, much less another living thing.

He wondered if he'd ever feel comfortable enough to tell Dori about his PTSD or to tell her how he loved her. Every day was a strain on his nerves, the need to be close to her warring with his need to be "whole" before he would even consider being with her.

Rubbing his hands through his hair to move it back into place, he stepped out of the truck and walked through the door into the chaos of feeding time at a dog rescue. Rina was filling dishes with food as his brother ferried them to individual kennels. He was relieved that Dori wasn't around. Each time he saw her, it ripped his heart a little further. He was making progress, but he was in no way ready to commit to her. Just the thought had his anxiety rising. He'd almost lost her once; he wasn't ready to take that chance again. Not yet, anyway.

His brother's voice brought his attention back to the scene in front of him. "About time you got here. You mind filling water dishes before you get started?"

"Sure. The forms for the concrete are almost done. It should take me about an hour to get those finished up and ready for the concrete to be poured tomorrow." Jessie stopped to admire the rebuilt shelter, his arms folded across his chest.

AJ smiled. "Looking good, isn't it? The renovations came together quickly. I was just telling Rina it looks better than it ever has. We'll be able to help so many dogs. And now with the expansion, Dori's going to make a real difference."

The addition would almost double the size of the shelter, giving ample room for Dori's new venture—training dogs to be companion and/or therapy animals. Jessie had been surprised when Rina told him about Dori's plans. She'd mentioned her experience training dogs before her ex had forbidden her from working outside their home, but she'd never mentioned wanting to train therapy dogs.

His mind wandered as he filled water dishes and carried them to the waiting dogs. How would a therapy dog help him? He knew about companion animals that helped disabled people with their daily lives, but he didn't see how that would translate to helping him with his PTSD. Maybe he should have paid more attention when his therapist had explained the benefits. With a sigh, he pulled out his phone and made a note to ask about it at his next appointment.

Once the dogs all had fresh water, he returned to his SUV and grabbed his toolbelt. Time to get to work and get those forms done.

The cool breeze ruffled his hair as he hammered nails and checked measurements, reminding him that fall weather would be arriving soon.

Intent on the job in front of him, he didn't notice the kids out in the field, setting off fireworks. Most of the noise battered at the edge of his consciousness until they set off an M-80, the boom resonating through him.

He dropped to the ground, the better to avoid enemy fire, crawling toward the remnants of a building that would provide some cover. The scene playing out in front of his eyes had nothing to do with his true surroundings. He was lost in his mind once again. With a yell to his team members, he waited for the next round of enemy fire. Usually after a missile, they sent in ground troops, but he didn't hear or see anyone, not even his own men. Where was everybody? How did he get out to the village?

Scanning the horizon, he heard a whine. Looking to his right, he found a stray dog huddled up against him, staring up at him with what looked like worry in its eyes. "Hey there, fella. What are you doing out here by yourself?"

Dropping his hand, he stroked the dogs head, trying to quiet him. The sound of a shoe kicking stones across the hard-packed sand of the village square had him bringing his weapon around and training on the sound. Seeing nothing, he resumed stroking the dog's head, relaxing as the scene before him wavered between the desert village of Afghanistan and the area around Rina's shelter. Realizing it was another episode, he sat up and hugged the dog, pressing his face into its fur to hide the tears. Would he ever feel normal again?

"Jessie?"

Automatically reaching for his weapon, he realized it wasn't a gun but an air hammer.

"You okay?"

Rubbing his face in the dog's fur, he mumbled, "Yeah. You just startled me."

Rina stared at him, accusation in her eyes. "When are you going to man up and tell me the truth? If that air hammer had been a rifle, you would have shot me." She lowered herself down and sat next to him, putting her hand on his face. "You need to get help."

"I am, but I'm still so broken. When will this all go away?" Tears silently slid down his cheeks. The dog whined, trying to lick his face. "What are you doing back here? I thought you had a new dog coming in."

Ruffling the fur around the dog's ears she explained, "This one here put up such a ruckus in his kennel that I was going to take him for a walk to calm him down. Reaching down to put the leash on him, I was distracted when I heard you yell, and he got away from me. I followed him out here to you, where I find you sprawled out in the dirt, hugging the dog. His name's Valiant, by the way."

"How did he know I needed help? Did you hear me yelling before that?"

"No, but he's one of Dori's therapy trainee dogs. He obviously is a quick study." With a smile, she pulled a treat out of her pocket and gave it to the dog. "Thanks, Valiant, for helping my friend Jessie. Good job." She stood and dusted off the seat of her jeans. "Did you really think I wouldn't notice you were having problems again? I remember how you were when you first moved here, and I can see that fear in your eyes again."

"Now do you understand why I can't be with Dori? She deserves someone who can protect her, not someone who has problems distinguishing fantasy from reality."

"Now that her ex is dead, she doesn't need to be protected. She needs to be loved."

Tired of everyone badgering him, he turned to look at Rina and yelled, "You think I don't know that? I love her more than anything, but I'm scared."

"We're all scared to expose our true selves, but we're better for it. Do you think it was easy for me to let you and AJ take care of me? The things my mother drilled into my head tried to keep me from letting AJ into my life as more than a friend."

"That doesn't scare me. I want to go up to her and tell her how much I love her, but I can't."

"Why not?"

"I might hurt her…physically."

"What?"

"Somehow, the PTSD is worse this time. Obviously AJ didn't tell you about the attack I had the day Dori came home from the hospital. When AJ found me in the state park, I was completely lost in my head." Turning away from her, he lowered his head and massaged the back of his neck. He turned and looked her in the eye as he whispered, "When he finally got through to me, I had my hands around his neck. If he hadn't been able to get through to me, I would have killed him. How can she love someone who is capable of killing their own brother?"

Chapter Thirteen

THE RUMBLE of the concrete mixer drowned out the barking of the dogs as it spit the sloppy mess into the forms, the late morning sun beating against Jessie's back. Shovel ready, he stood prepared to help spread the concrete into every corner of the forms. The mindless task allowed him to think about his relationship with Dori. The thought of letting her go permanently made it hard for him to breathe, as if she was the air he pulled into his lungs. Rina's reaction when he told her about the episode with AJ made him question his reasoning. First she'd hugged him, crying at his heartbreak. And then she punched him for not telling her. He had a feeling his brother got a similar punch when Rina caught up with him. His jaw was still sore the next morning. AJ's woman packed a punch. But it was the hug that convinced him to give the situation some more thought. Could a loving relationship actually help with his issues and not cause more problems?

Once the concrete had been poured and leveled, he was done for the day.

"Hey, Jess."

He looked up to find Dori standing in the doorway, looking at the area that would be her training ring. "Beauty."

"Why do you still call me that? It's obvious you don't think that's true any longer."

Mentally kicking himself in the ass, he vowed to himself that he was telling her the whole truth right now. "I...uh..." Taking a swig from the water bottle in his hand, he braced himself and dove in. "We need to talk. Would you walk with me back to my place?"

"Okay. Let me go tell Rina I'm leaving."

Wiping his palms on his shorts, he hoped she would be open to hearing his truth. He'd been sidestepping his issues and telling her half-truths for a month, and he regretted the lies. She deserved a man who could and would be truthful.

"You ready?"

He turned to find her standing near him, her face even more beautiful than before. How could he tell her just how broken he was?

"Thank you for all the work you're doing at the shelter."

"It's keeping me busy." Mental head slap. *Tell her the truth, dummy*, he thought to himself. "Actually, it's been therapeutic for me. I took a leave from my job at the suggestion of my therapist, not because of cutbacks."

Dori stopped in front of him. "It's about time you told me the truth."

"There's so much more to it. I've been having some PTSD episodes, and I thought I could deal with them by myself. After a particularly bad episode, AJ convinced me to see someone about them."

"You think I didn't know? I could see it in your eyes, the doubt and the fear. It's the same look I see when I look in the mirror."

He picked up her hand and held it, rubbing his thumb

across the back. "Every time you flinched when I touched you, the doubts would creep in, increasing my anxiety and bringing on episodes. And then you were taken from me."

"You know that had nothing to do with you, right? It was all about Ty's need to control me. If you hadn't found me when you did, he would have killed me. He left marks on me where others could see. He wasn't planning on letting me out of that shack, not alive anyway."

He pulled her into him, wrapping his arms around her and burying his face in her hair, the memory of the nightmare making him want to be sick. "I want you to know I love you." He stared into her eyes, watching for them to change as he continued. "But I can't be the man you need right now."

She cupped his cheek with her hand. "That's bullshit. You've always been the man I need even when I didn't know it. I need a man who loves me, not one who is perfect. There's no such person." Pulling him into a hug, she whispered, "I love you, not how you can protect me or what you can provide for me."

Hugging her close, he battled to keep from tearing himself away from her. He didn't deserve the love she had for him. "I get that, but…"

"But what?" Backing out of his embrace, she stared at him. "We both have issues to work through, and I want nothing more than to put these things behind us and move forward, but it's not going to be easy."

"I'm terrified I'll hurt you. When I'm in the grip of an episode, I have no control over my actions. I'm reacting to what my mind throws at me, not what's actually happening. If I did something that hurt you, I would never be able to forgive myself."

"That works both ways, Marine. Who's to say I won't react to something and respond without thinking. What if I'm holding a knife and I stab you?" Rubbing her hands up and down her arms, she thrust the image of a bleeding Jessie out of her mind. "What I'm getting at is life is uncertain even under the best of circumstances. If we wait until we are both 'healed' or whatever, we'll probably never find true happiness. Letting someone into my heart after how Ty twisted our love to suit his sick needs terrifies me, but I'm putting myself out there for you. I believe in you, in us, that we can overcome our issues and be happy together."

Taking her hand, he pulled her up under his arm so he could hold her as they walked. "I have another confession to make. That first day after I changed your tire, I stopped by the jewelry store on my way back to Rina's and bought a ring. Even back then, I knew you were the one. No matter how much I fought it or tried to bury those feelings, I always had that in the back of my mind." Steering her down the path, he felt freer than he had in months. Anxiety be damned, he was going to enjoy life for a change and not worry about what might happen.

"So, don't you have anything else to say?"

"What? Pledging my undying love wasn't enough for you?" he asked with a grin.

"You bought a ring, which I already knew anyway. I saw it on your dresser before all hell broke loose. Aren't you going to ask me a question?"

"Now? Out here? I was going to wait for the perfect time."

"Seriously, didn't you just get done talking about how you were done waiting?"

Picking her up and swinging her around, he laughed. "I love how you're not afraid to speak your mind with me." Setting her on her feet, he took a deep breath to calm his racing heart. How did he get so lucky to find his Beauty? He patted his pants, grateful he'd tucked the ring in his pocket just as he'd done every day since he bought it. She was right; there was no moment more perfect than now. Dropping down to one knee, he acted like he was tying his shoe, snickering when he heard her sigh.

"Seriously, you didn't just drop to one knee and then tie your shoe."

Looking at her beautiful, annoyed face, he grinned. "Just had to see what you'd do." Taking her hand in his, he poured out everything he'd been burying over the last couple of months. "I've been broken for so long, but for some insane reason, you think I'm fixable. Your love is the glue holding me together. Will you glue me together forever and marry me?"

He watched as she blinked, big, fat tears dropping from her eyes.

"Beauty, what's wrong? Geez, how did I manage to screw this up?"

"Hearing you finally admit how you feel…it's amazing. I'd hoped the love I saw in your eyes was real, but those words… Beautiful."

"And here I thought AJ got all the pretty words." With a laugh, he stood and pulled her into his arms. "But seriously, don't leave me hanging. Will you marry me, my Beauty?"

"Yes, yes, yes!"

Slipping the ring on her finger, he knew no matter the obstacles, they would make it through, together.

Chapter Fourteen

NINE MONTHS LATER...

Valiant trotting by his side, Jessie jogged up the drive toward Rina's dog rescue and his duties as spokesman for Beyond Duty, the not-for-profit portion of Dori's dog training business that provided therapy and companion animals for returning vets.

AJ called to him from the porch. "Hey, Jess, I've got news about the book."

After a couple of stretches, Jessie picked up his niece from the bassinette next to his brother's chair and sat opposite his twin as he motioned for Valiant to sit. "Good news, I hope. Dori's been hinting that she wants to redecorate, and I'm going to need some extra cash to make that happen." He smiled as the baby gurgled at him. "You love your Uncle Jessie best, don't you, sweet girl?"

"Well, the book went live this morning, and it's already moving up the charts. It's getting great reviews, and Robert has even gotten some inquiries about having you do custom photos for some other authors. Looks like you'll have the money for those redecorating costs and a sizeable donation for Beyond Duty. Good job, brother."

"Custom photo shoots? Is that even a thing?"

"Oh yeah. Authors want their covers to stand out, and they must think you have the right look to do that. My brother, the model!"

"Who would have thought writing out my story as a part of my therapy would end up starting me on a possible new career path as a hunk of beefcake. Thanks for the update. I need to go tell Beauty." With a huge grin, he kissed his niece before laying her back down. With a whistle for Valiant, he walked toward the barn that housed the rescue and dog training facilities.

"Dori? Where are you, beautiful?"

He heard shuffling and a door slam. Rina walked out from the office area, looking at her feet instead of up at him.

"What's wrong? Is it Dori?"

He stormed past her, not waiting for her to answer. Raising his fist, he banged on Dori's office door. "Beauty, what's wrong?"

"Nothing. I'll be out in a minute."

Rattling the doorknob, he was shocked to discover the door was locked. He was surprised it even had a lock on it. "Dori, honey, why is the door locked? Open up, or I'm busting it down."

The lock clicked open, and he turned the knob. Reminding himself to breathe, he pushed the door open to find his Beauty sitting cross-legged in her chair, using a tissue to frantically wipe at her face.

Dropping to his knees in front of her chair, he pulled her into his arms. "What's wrong, my Beauty? Who made you cry?"

"You did."

"What? What did I do?" He thought back over the last couple of days and remembered nothing that should have evoked this reaction.

"You knocked me up!"

"But I didn't mean… What? You're pregnant?"

"Congrats, Papa."

He sat as his knees collapsed under him. They were both doing so much better, but were they ready for a baby? Holy shit, a BABY!

About the Author

Romance author, dialysis warrior, furkid mom, and Best Fiends addict. Lover of coffee, 80's music, and all things romance. During the day she carves out writing time in between trips to the back door as doorman to her four-legged furry child. At night after spending quality time with her husband she chips away at her never-ending TBR pile.

Keep up with Hoosiergirl Publishing here:
https://hoosiergirl-publishing.kit.com/df28902ff9

You can find all her links on her website:
https://www.laremenicky.com

Also by L.A. REMENICKY

Next Up In The Fairfield Corners Series

Ragan's Song (Fairfield Corners Book 2) – It only took one look into his eyes for her to know she was in trouble. Adam Bricklin has heard the melody in his head for years, the one that told him if a decision was right or wrong.

When he met Ragan Newlin, the song told him she was the one. He was devastated when circumstances tore them apart.

It took three years for Adam to finally move past the heartbreak he suffered when Ragan left town in the middle of the night. No note, no email, no text. She was just gone.

Now he had a new girlfriend, a new album was in the works, and his daughter was doing well in school. Then Ragan returned to Fairfield Corners. Ragan came home to celebrate her parents' anniversary, hoping they would forgive her for not telling them about her marriage or her son.

When she discovered Adam was still living in Fairfield Corners, she hoped her secrets were safe. Those secrets drove her away three years ago and could change their lives forever.

https://books2read.com/RagansSong

Also from the Lavish Publishing family

SAMANTHA JACOBEY

Rendered (Irrevocable Series Book 1)
Samantha Jacobey
https://books2read.com/Rendered

The end of the world is coming, or so they say, and that puts Bailey Dewitt on a crash course with Armageddon. Orphaned, she and her young brothers find themselves living with their renegade uncle as part of a group of survivalists. She struggles against them, searching for a way to escape, but every discovery only terrifies her more.

For Caleb Cross, the Ranch is a way of life. The members of their group are family, and none should come between them. Smitten from the moment he met Bailey, his choices are no longer easy, his path no longer clear. He wants to welcome her and the twins into their fold and hopes his kin will agree.

But the elders who lead them aren't interested in the troublesome girl. They are plotting for the time they will be rid of her and expect Caleb to go along with their plans - he is after all one of them.

At first, Bailey resists Caleb's charms, but soon must admit that she desperately needs a friend. She has no intention of anything more, but when the elders make their move, she is forced to trust him with her very life.

They both have hard lessons to learn. Relationships built on secrets and lies don't come with guarantees. When the world falls apart around them, some things are Irrevocable.

Realistic sci-fi and romantic suspense will pull you into to the first book of the Irrevocable Trilogy.

Summer's Deceit (The Trilogy Book 1)
Sara J. Bernhardt
https://books2read.com/SummersDeceit

Jane Callahan is a reclusive, seventeen-year-old high school student dealing with the death of her beloved brother. Her home in Southern California with her mother is a constant reminder of her loss and pain. In hopes of escaping her past she moves to North Bend Oregon to live with her father, where she meets a beautiful boy named Aidan Summers.

Jane is intrigued by his looks as well as his unusual ways of attempting to get her attention. After months of uncommon conversation and frustration, an uncertain romance brews between Jane and Aidan, but Aidan has a ghastly secret that could destroy everything.

Get swept away by The Hunter's Trilogy – YA romantic suspense with a paranormal twist.